★ American Girl®

Blaire
COOKS UP A PLAN

BY JENNIFER CASTLE

Scholastic Inc.

Published by Scholastic Inc., *Publishers since 1920*. SCHOLASTIC and associated logos are trademarks and/or registered trademarks of Scholastic Inc.

The publisher does not have any control over and does not assume any responsibility for author or third-party websites or their content.

This book is a work of fiction. Names, characters, places, and incidents are either the product of the author's imagination or are used fictitiously, and any resemblance to actual persons, living or dead, business establishments, events, or locales is entirely coincidental and not intended by American Girl or Scholastic Inc.

Book design by Suzanne LaGasa

© 2019 American Girl. All American Girl marks, Blaire™, Blaire Wilson™, and Girl of the Year™ are trademarks of American Girl. Used under license by Scholastic Inc.

Safety note: Even though instructions have been tested and results from testing were incorporated into this book, all recommendations and suggestions are made without any guarantees on the part of American Girl. Because of different tools, materials, ingredients, conditions, and individual skills, the publisher disclaims liability for any injuries, losses, or other damages that may result from using the information in the book. Knives, ovens and stoves, hot dishes and ingredients, uncooked food, and powered appliances can cause severe injury. ***Adult supervision is required at all times when following any instruction in this book.***

americangirl.com/service

ISBN 978-1-338-26718-1

10 9 8 7 6 5 4 3 2 1   19 20 21 22 23

Printed in the U.S.A.   23 • First printing 2019

FOR MY GRANDMOTHER SADYE GARONZIK,
WHO SHOWED ME WHAT IT MEANS TO
TRULY MAKE A DIFFERENCE

–J.C.

Contents

CHAPTER 1

Kids in Pajamas

*Y*ou learn something new every day.

That's what Grandpa always says. Here's my something-new for today:

It's not easy to put pajamas on a baby goat.

"Dash! Sit still!" I scolded this particular goat. Dash was a four-month-old kid, brown with a thick black stripe down his back. Right now, though, he was acting more like an octopus, wriggling his little hooves as I tried to slip them into the pajamas. His best friend, our lamb Penelope, was already prancing around their pen in her pink-flowered pj's. At least *she* recognized a fashion Do when she saw it.

My own (human) best friend, Thea, knelt down beside me. "Need help? Two human kids should be able to get one goat kid into pajamas."

"Yes, please!" I laughed, and she held Dash gently,

rubbing his soft ears. It took a few more minutes, but Thea and I finally managed to get tops and bottoms on this goat. "Whew," I said as Dash squirmed out of our arms. "*That* was a workout I didn't expect."

"Purple polka dots are so *you*, Dash," Thea said as he raced to the other side of the pen.

"Comfy, right?"

In the coop next to the pen, the chickens clucked loudly. I wasn't sure if they approved or if they were laughing at Dash. He didn't seem to care. He bounced up onto a hay bale and then jumped down to the ground. Up onto the hay, then down again. It was like he had springs in his legs. Dash ran over to Penny and they sniffed each other's pajamas before he started chasing her around the toddler-sized play set we'd put in their pen. Penny jumped to the top of the plastic slide and skittered. Dash followed.

"Looks like it's thumbs-up on the pj's," I told Thea. "Or, I guess, *hooves* up."

"Too. Much. Cuteness," Thea said in her robot voice. "System. Overload. May. Explode."

"I didn't know I'd be *sew* successful," I told Thea, spelling out my joke for her. "The pj's were just a fun project with all my spare time after Cat and Gabe's wedding."

Caterina Minardi was our farm manager. She and her fiancé, Gabe, had just gotten married in the renovated barn here at Pleasant View Farm, my home and my family's business. Cat felt like a member of our family, and I was thrilled when she'd let me help her plan the wedding. But once the wedding was over, I had a *lot* of time on my hands. So my hands made pajamas, from an idea I got watching an online video about creating kids' pj's from old blankets.

Baaaaah.

Penny was standing between me and Thea, giving us the lamb version of the stink-eye.

"What is it, Penny?" I asked. "Are you mad that we're not in our pajamas, too?"

"We'll take care of that right away," Thea added, and we both climbed into the two-person tent my dad had set up on the lawn just outside the animal pen.

This wasn't just a pajama party . . . it was a sleepover with a lamb and a goat.

"I'm so happy we're finally doing this!" Thea said as she pulled a pajama top over her head. "No more wedding craziness."

I nodded. I'd been promising Thea we'd do this sleepover for two months—ever since my family adopted Dash and Penny. But then Cat and Gabe's big event took over my life.

"Better September than never," I said. "But you have to admit, that wedding was *fun!*"

"The wedding, yes," Thea agreed. "The planning? Not so much."

"Well, things are back to normal now," I said as we finished changing and climbed out of the tent. "It's just you and me and a couple of baby animals in pj's."

Penny and Dash were still hopping around the pen.

"Hey!" Thea shouted at them. "You guys started the dance party without us? How dare you!" She turned and pointed at me. "Cue the sleepover soundtrack."

I grabbed my tablet, found the music playlist I'd made for this special occasion, and turned the volume all the way up.

Thea and I shimmied and shook. Penny and Dash boomeranged back and forth across the pen, which was *obviously* the goat and lamb version of dancing. I stood Penny up on her hind legs, holding her front ones so it looked like we were doing a waltz. We took about a zillion selfies with the animals and sent them to our friends.

After a couple of songs, Dash and Penny made a beeline for their water trough. Thea and I collapsed into a pile of hay.

"Best . . . dance party . . . ever," Thea gasped as she tried to catch her breath.

Baaaah, Penny agreed.

"Um, why are the animals wearing pajamas?" a voice above us asked.

I looked up to see my little brother, Beckett, standing outside the pen in a sequined silver vest and a black top hat.

"Um, what are *you* wearing?" I asked, sitting up.

"This is my costume," Beckett said. "Dad said Dash could be the main attraction at our booth for the Bluefield Harvest Festival. I've got two weeks to work on our act." Beckett straightened his hat. "Can I show you the tricks we've got so far?"

"Go for it," I said, then whispered to Thea, "This should be good."

As Beckett opened the gate, he pulled a container of licorice-flavored goat treats out of his pocket and shook them. Dash rushed over to Beckett as if someone had just flipped Dash's *On* switch.

"Okay, Dash," Beckett said. "First, give me a high five."

Beckett held out his hand, and Dash put one of his hooves in Beckett's palm.

"Good boy!" Beckett gave Dash a treat as Thea and I raised our eyebrows at each other. "Now," continued Beckett, "show me your best goat disco moves."

This time Beckett held his hand way above his head and started walking backward. Dash stood up on his hind legs and "danced" as he followed Beckett.

"That's a pretty great move," Thea whispered to me. "What should we call it?"

"Maybe instead of the 'Nae Nae,' this could be the 'Maaaah Maaaah,'" I murmured back.

While Thea and I were giggling, Beckett was still backing up. And since he'd left the gate to the pen open, he was headed right for our tent.

"Watch out—" I called, just as my brother tripped on one of the tent cords and stumbled through the opening. A half second later, Dash jumped over him and into the tent.

"Help!" Beckett whimpered, struggling to untangle himself from the tent cord. His hat fell off, and Dash took a bite of the rim. "My magic hat!" Beckett cried.

I helped Beckett with the cord and pulled him to his feet. But when I crawled into the tent to get Dash, I couldn't find him.

"Well, Beckett, it looks like that hat still has magic," I called. "You made Dash disappear."

"Huh?" Beckett asked, poking his head into the tent.

There was no goat.

But suddenly, there was a lamb. Penny had nosed her way inside, past Beckett, and was sniffing around. Beckett climbed in after her. We were definitely pushing the limits of the "two-person" part of this tent.

Then I saw Thea's sleeping bag move.

"Dash!"

I grabbed at the bag, but Dash had squirmed his way to the bottom, twisting it up as he went along.

"Thea! We need backup!" I called.

Thea rushed into the tent. Beckett held the Dash-lump still while Thea and I tried to untwist and unzip the sleeping bag. But as soon as we made enough room for Dash to crawl out of the bag, Penny started to crawl in.

"Thea, grab Penny!" I shouted.

When I managed to completely unzip the bag, there was Dash, with Thea's pillow in his mouth. Well, part of a pillow.

"Bad goat," I scolded, pulling the pillow away from him.

Dash hopped out of the tent, and Penny trotted after him.

Thea and I looked at Beckett.

"That," said Beckett, "is not part of the act."

⁂

The sun was starting to set behind the Shawangunk Ridge in the distance, and the air felt cooler, crisper. I loved fall in Bluefield, our corner of New York's Hudson Valley. I couldn't wait for the leaves to start changing colors, and for many of the fruits and vegetables we grew to be ready for harvesting, cooking, and sharing.

After we sent Beckett and his magic hat back to the house and got Thea a new sleeping bag and pillow, we took the pj's off Penny and Dash and tucked them into their shed for the night.

"One tent, two people," Thea said as we crawled into our tent.

"What a concept," I replied, turning on the battery-powered lantern. The window flaps were up, and we could hear crickets and cicadas singing their familiar chorus. We flopped onto our sleeping bags, and Thea rolled toward me, propping her head on one elbow.

"Um, you have hay in your hair," I said.

"You too," she replied. "It's barnyard bedhead. Wanna play Best and Worst?"

"Sure," I replied. "You go first."

Thea thought for a moment. "Best and Worst things about fifth grade so far." She rolled onto her back and stared at the top of the tent before continuing. "Best: Rosie, Amadi, and Sabrina are all in our class this year. We're going to have a blast. Worst: We're going to get more homework. And it sounds like our projects will be harder."

"But they sound like fun, too," I said. "I can't wait to start the Fifth-Grade Community Service Challenge."

Thea rolled back to face me, her eyes lighting up. "Remember my cousin George and his Challenge project—Cans for a Cause? Not only did he collect a thousand cans of dog food for the animal shelter, but he stacked them in the shape of a doghouse."

"How could I forget? We've been walking by that framed newspaper article about him every day since second grade!"

Right inside the entrance to Bluefield Elementary, there was a COMMUNITY SERVICE ALL-STARS display case, showing the volunteer projects over the years that were unique or made an extra-big difference. When we got to school last week, there was a sign above the case that read, HEY, FIFTH-GRADE LEADERS! READY TO RISE TO THE CHALLENGE THIS YEAR?

"It would be awesome to see our projects on display," I said.

"Definitely," Thea agreed. "But we have to come up with projects first. Hey—maybe we could make a thousand pairs of animal pajamas!"

I laughed. "That would be one way to leave a mark on the community."

"Okay," Thea said. "Your turn. Best and Worst."

"Best is easy. Ms. Lewis is a really cool teacher."

We'd been back at school for only a few days, but I already knew she was great. She'd made a gift bag for every kid in the class with clues to what we'd be learning this year, like polar bear pencils and fraction dominoes.

"My Worst is . . ." I paused, because I hadn't told Thea my news yet. "My Worst is having to get used to eating dairy-free at school."

"What do you mean?" Thea asked, giving me a confused look. "I thought you were just on a trial for the summer."

"I was," I said, flopping onto my back. "I went back to the doctor last week, and she gave me the go-ahead to eat dairy again."

"Seriously?" Thea sat up. "That's great," she cried.

"It would have been great if I didn't get sick right away. I had some of Mom's homemade macaroni and cheese, and after I ate it, I got cramps and ended up in the bathroom for an hour. I tried some ice cream a few days later, and the same thing happened."

"Oh"—Thea's shoulders slumped forward—"so no dairy ever?"

I sat up and hugged my knees to my chest. "Not for the foreseeable future. That's what the doctor said. My lactose intolerance is bad enough that even a little bit will make me feel rotten. So no dairy for now."

"Oh, Blaire, that stinks," Thea said. "I'm sorry."

"Thanks," I said. "I was hoping I could just go back to eating anything I wanted."

"But it *has* gotten easier to avoid dairy, right?" Thea asked.

I shrugged. At the beginning of summer, when I was first diagnosed, it was really hard to be dairy-free. "Yeah, it's definitely easier here at home. But school . . . well, it's . . ."

"It's *school*," Thea said. "I get it."

I nodded. "I know *you* do. But other kids don't. I know they're going to ask questions, and I just don't like to talk about it . . ." I let my voice trail off. I didn't even like to talk about it with Thea.

"I bet no one will even notice," Thea said kindly.

"They will when I say 'no, thanks' to someone's birthday cookies. It's going to be so obvious."

"It doesn't have to be," Thea insisted. "It's not like you won't be eating anything. Your mom sent in all those dairy-free snacks. You'll just eat those. No biggie."

I sighed. No biggie for her. "I just wanted this to magically go away." I flopped down onto my sleeping bag and covered my face with my pillow.

Thea lifted up a corner of my pillow. "You could try Beckett's magic hat. If it can make a goat disappear, who knows what else it can do."

MAAAAH.

Dash bleated from inside the shed as though he'd been listening. Thea and I burst out laughing.

"So much for magic," I said.

JMGG

I woke to the sound of chickens clucking. I was used to hearing them from my third-floor bedroom, but sleeping right next to the coop was a whole new experience. I stretched and listened to the morning music of their squawks and calls.

Thea sat up, rubbing her eyes. "What is all that racket?"

"It's the Pleasant View Farm wake-up call," I told her. "Isn't it great?"

"No. It's early," Thea said with a yawn.

"Well, Penny and Dash are up." I heard them rattling the door of their shed. "Want to help me feed them?"

Thea and I pulled on work boots before letting Penny and Dash out into their pen. I gave them hay while Thea filled the trough with fresh water. Then we scattered seed for the chickens.

"Is it time for *us* to eat now?" Thea asked.

"Yes! Let's grab some eggs and make breakfast."

At my house, "grab some eggs" means getting them fresh from the nests. As we made our way to the indoor nesting boxes, I picked up my favorite chicken, a Silkie I'd named Dandelion because of the way the feathers on her head poufed out like dandelion fluff.

I nuzzled her soft, warm body. "Next time, we'll have a dance party with you guys, promise," I whispered to her.

Dandy clucked as if to say, *Don't you dare try to put me in pajamas.*

"Blaire, your bedhead makes you and Dandelion look like twins," Thea teased.

We gathered as many eggs as we could hold in our pajama tops and headed toward the house. I could smell something great coming from the kitchen: Mom making breakfast for the B-and-B guests.

My mom is an amazing cook—she's the chef at our farm-to-table restaurant. She taught me everything I know about cooking. This morning I was going to create a feast for Thea and me.

"What'll it be?" I asked Thea as we approached the big front porch. "Omelette? Frittata? Oh—I just found a new recipe for almond milk french toast."

Before Thea could answer, there was a roar from the road. We turned to see a motorcycle zooming up the driveway. The bike was bright red and the rider was wearing a red leather suit and matching red helmet.

"Well, that's something you don't see every day," Thea muttered next to me.

Actually, it wasn't that unusual. Between the restaurant and the B and B, there were all sorts of vehicles appearing in my driveway. Every day, someone new and interesting showed up at Pleasant View Farm. I loved getting to know our guests.

The motorcycle came to a stop, and the rider climbed off.

"Good morning!" a man's voice called from inside the helmet. It sounded oddly familiar, but I didn't know anyone who rode a red motorcycle. Who *was* this?

Then he pulled off his helmet.

OH. MY. GOSH.

CHAPTER 2

Super-Bonita!

N o. Way," Thea whispered next to me. "Is that really . . ."

"Marco Gonzalez," I finished.

OMG, times a million. Marco Gonzalez's online video channel, *Room Revolutions*, is one of our favorites. He's a designer who always comes up with something that makes you go, *Whoa!*

Marco smiled wide, put his helmet down on the seat of the motorcycle, and began walking toward us.

"Uh, Blaire," Thea murmured to me. "FYI, you now have hay *and* chicken feathers in your hair."

"I do?" I wanted to brush my hand through my hair, but I was holding the corners of my shirt to cradle the eggs.

OMG. Not a shirt! A pajama top!

I felt heat rush straight from my feet up to the back

of my neck. My favorite celebrity designer had appeared at my front porch . . . and here I was *in my pj's and dirty work boots*. With hay and feathers in my hair.

"A *fantastico* morning to you!" Marco said.

"Hi!" I said, suddenly nervous. "Welcome to Pleasant View Farm!"

"I'm humbled to be here. My name is Marco."

"I know . . . we're, uh . . . big fans," I said. "I'm Blaire, and this is my friend . . ."

"Theodora Dimitriou," Thea said, in the most grown-up voice I'd ever heard her do. Since she couldn't shake his hand, she raised her egg-filled pajama top as if it were a ball gown and curtsied. "Charmed."

Marco bowed deeply from the waist. "Miss Dimitriou," he replied. Turning to me, he said, "Miss Wilson. Young event designer. It's an honor to meet you."

Wait. Marco Gonzalez knows my name? And he called me *an event designer!*

Marco looked at our big Victorian house, nodding his approval. "This is a stunning home, like a work of art. Built in the 1880s, yes?" Then he turned to the freshly painted barn down the hill. "And the renovated barn looks just *perfecto!*"

"You've heard about that, too?" I asked.

"Oh yes, I've read all about it!" he said, then smiled, a twinkle in his eye. "Thanks to *Empire State Weddings.*"

"Whoa!" I exclaimed. "The new issue is finally out?" A writer from the magazine had come to Cat's wedding to take pictures and write about our event space. We'd been anxiously waiting to see it. "What does the review say?"

"I have an advance copy right here," Marco said, tapping his saddlebag. "And the review is . . . wonderful!"

"Wonderful? Really? Wow . . . that's so . . . exciting!" I stammered.

"I'm just starting a renovation at a historic house in Bluefield," Marco said. "When I read this article and saw the photos, I had to come see Pleasant View Farm for myself. Perhaps someone could show me around?"

"Absolutely!" a voice said from the porch. It was Dad. Grandpa stepped out of the house behind him. "I'm Daniel Wilson. This is my father-in-law, Ben O'Connell."

"This is Magazine—er, Marco!" I said. "He has an advance copy of the motorcycle. I mean, magazine! With the Pleasant View Farm review in it!"

Grandpa came down the steps carrying a wire basket. "I saw you from inside, Blaire. It looks like you need a bit of help," he said, unloading the eggs from my shirt. He winked at me before gathering the eggs that Thea was holding.

Grandpa left the eggs on the porch, and Dad led the way to the barn as he explained all the renovations we'd done.

"Blaire helped me plan the space," he said, "and she put in a lot of elbow grease to have it ready in time for Cat's big day."

Marco smiled at me. "Way to go, elbows."

I blushed. "Thea helped, too. She even made up a rap while we were working."

"*You wanna have a wedding where it's warm and cozy?*" Thea began to rap, throwing herself into the performance. "*Come party right here, and everything will be rosy!*"

Marco laughed and started dancing to her song. "I love it," he said as we got to the barn.

"We're working on decorations for a one-hundredth-birthday party next weekend," I said, sliding the door open and ushering Marco inside.

"*SUPER-BONITA!*" he exclaimed, and Thea and I couldn't help giggling. That's a catchphrase he uses when he thinks something really works.

And it did look *super-bonita*. I pointed to the ceiling and told Marco we'd tied exactly one hundred white ribbons above us to make a canopy over the space. There were ten tables, and each represented a different decade. I'd finished a few of the centerpieces. The one for the 1920s was gold and black, with feather boas and toy jazz instruments. The 1950s table had a mini-jukebox and old records, and the 1970s was all tie-dye and peace signs.

"Grandpa and I researched the decades," I told Marco.

"Oh excellent, that's fun, fun, fun. I like this a thousand percent," Marco said, circling the tables and taking it all in. "You've put so much creative thought into this event."

Thea nudged me and grinned. I grinned back. Here was a professional designer I really admired, saying nice things about my ideas!

Marco wanted to see the rest of the farm, so we led him past the herb and kitchen gardens. We showed him the growing fields and greenhouse in the distance, then walked under the white wooden arch to the orchard, to the gazebo by the creek where Cat and Gabe's wedding ceremony was held.

When we got to the animals, Marco fell in love with the chickens. "These Silkies have style!" he exclaimed. "Pleasant View Farms is even better in person. It feels *mágico*."

"Thank you," Dad said. "Do you have time to come in and have some breakfast?"

"I always have time for breakfast. And I can show you the magazine review!"

"Finally!" Thea cried, saying what I was thinking.

In the restaurant dining room, we introduced Marco to Mom. I saw my mother blush for the first time in, like, ever. She *loves* watching *Room Revolutions* with me.

Thea and I whipped up some eggs while Mom made apple pancakes. We all sat at a big wooden table on the restaurant patio. While we ate, Marco spread open the *Empire State Weddings* issue. There it all was: photos of the ceremony at the gazebo by the creek, Cat and Gabe riding a tandem bicycle down the pathway lined with luminarias, the barn at sunset, a table setting with

Mom's beautifully plated meal, Gabe's mother's bubble machine, and Cat and Gabe holding a pair of chickens dressed like a bride and groom.

When we told Marco the story of the chickens invading the barn, he was delighted. "You know what I always say," Marco exclaimed. "If there's no drama—"

"There's no fun!" Thea and I finished one of his favorite sayings for him.

"This is such a great review," Mom said as she read through the article. I could hear both excitement and relief in her voice.

"I couldn't have wished for better," Dad agreed, putting his arm around her.

"You know, Marco," Grandpa said. "It was my idea to restore the barn and start hosting big events."

Marco looked confused when Mom, Dad, Thea, and I burst out laughing. "Grandpa was dead set against the barn all summer," I explained to Marco. "He didn't come around to the idea until he saw how wonderful Cat and Gabe's wedding turned out."

Marco clapped Grandpa gently on the back. "Well, whoever had the idea, it was a good one. Marco's prediction: Your farm will be busy with big events for a long time."

"More decorating!" I announced.

"Slow down, junior designer," Dad said. "It was one thing to help with Cat's wedding during the summer. You're in school now. That's your priority."

"And you still have plenty of chores," Mom reminded me.

"Don't be sad," Marco said. "You get to *live* here! I wish I could stay here instead of at some boring hotel."

Grandpa pulled a chicken feather from my hair. "It's almost never boring around here."

"We just had a cancellation for one of our rooms," Dad said, "so you *could* stay here."

At exactly the same time, Marco, Thea, and I said, "*Super-bonita!*"

"Jinx!" Marco said to me and Thea. Then he turned to Dad. "That's an offer I won't turn down. *Muchas gracias.*" Marco jumped up from his chair. "Excuse me while I go call my producer. She'll take care of the arrangements." Marco headed inside, but he paused at the door and turned back to Thea and me. "Would you girls like to come visit the house I'm renovating?"

My mouth dropped open. "That. Would. Be. Awesome."

Marco nodded and left. I turned to Thea. "I can't believe it. *Room Revolutions* is working on a house right here in Bluefield AND we're going to visit the set AND Marco Gonzalez is staying at Pleasant View Farm!"

"Believe it, *dahling*," Thea said. "But say good-bye to things getting back to normal."

CHAPTER 3

Monday Madness

Ms. Lewis clapped her hands three times.

"Ready to rock?" she called.

Everyone in our class clapped three times and shouted back, "Ready to roll!"

"Okay!" she said. "Monday Madness starts now!"

Every Monday morning, Ms. Lewis lets us have a party to talk about what was going to happen during the week at school. She said she didn't know why everyone always had class celebrations on Fridays, because Mondays were when you really needed a party. "Besides, our classroom is a community," she explained. "And our community needs a chance to connect before starting the week."

Today, Amadi, Rosie, Sabrina, Thea, and I came together instantly, like magnets, and flopped onto a pile of pillows in the corner.

"I still can't believe Marco from *Room Revolutions* is

staying at your B and B," Amadi said to me. "That is epic! When can I meet him?"

"And when will there be another animal pajama party?" Sabrina asked.

Before I could answer, there was a knock on the classroom door.

"Perfect timing," Ms. Lewis said as she got up to open it. "We're getting a new student."

Everyone turned to see our principal, Ms. Cheeger, walk in with a boy. He had dark hair and was wearing a T-shirt with a cartoon of a cat eating a taco. It read TACOCAT SPELLED BACKWARD IS TACOCAT.

"Good morning, kids!" Ms. Cheeger announced. "I'd like to introduce you to Eli Carr. Eli just moved here from California. I hope you'll all make him feel very welcome at Bluefield Elementary."

"Hi, Eli," I said, with a wave. "Welcome." Everyone else did the same kind of thing. But Eli just stared at the floor.

Ms. Lewis went over to Eli and offered her hand. "Eli, I'm Ms. Lewis. So happy to meet you!"

Eli finally looked up, shook Ms. Lewis's hand, then scanned the room. He didn't smile or meet anyone's eye.

"It must be freaky, being the new kid," Thea murmured to me.

"Yeah," I whispered back. "Especially with everyone staring at you. I'd be nervous."

Thea and I had lived in Bluefield our whole lives. I couldn't imagine what it would be like to walk into a classroom full of strangers.

After Ms. Cheeger left, Ms. Lewis led Eli to the carpet and said, "Eli, would you like to share a fun fact about yourself?"

Eli's eyes traveled all over our classroom, taking in the posters on the walls and the giant solar system Ms. Lewis had hung from the ceiling. Then he sighed as his gaze settled on the big map of the United States above the whiteboard. "Okay. I've lived in eight different states, and I've visited seventeen others."

Whoa. That's a lot of traveling. I'd only ever been to Massachusetts, Pennsylvania, and New Jersey. Living on a farm, and running a restaurant and B and B, meant that my family stayed close to home. I *felt* like I traveled a lot because I spent so much time talking to our guests about where they were from. But Eli was a true traveler. I couldn't wait to ask him about that.

"That *is* a fun fact, Eli," Ms. Lewis said. "I hope you'll tell us more soon. Now find yourself a spot on the carpet. We were just about to have a snack."

My stomach twisted. This was the moment I was dreading.

Ms. Lewis said, "We're all taking turns bringing the Monday Madness snack, and Joey is starting us off."

As Joey jumped up to get a paper grocery bag from his cubby, Ms. Lewis turned to me and said, "Blaire, would you help me with napkins?"

I got up and followed her to the back of the room. "I want to show you where I keep the items your mom sent in," Ms. Lewis said quietly. "Feel free to come get these any time you need to switch out a snack, okay?"

Ms. Lewis opened a cabinet, and there were the dairy-free cookies and granola bars Mom had bought, plus some of the trail mix we make at home. "Thanks," I whispered. I grabbed a stack of napkins and looked to see what Joey had brought.

Two boxes of bright orange cheese crackers, filled with cheese spread.

A definite no for me.

I sighed, turned back to the cabinet, and pulled the

container of trail mix from the shelf. I put the napkins on top, hoping no one would notice my separate snack.

"Do you want to tell the class about your lactose intolerance?" Ms. Lewis asked quietly.

I shook my head quickly. "Maybe some other time."

Ms. Lewis smiled and squeezed my shoulder. "You just let me know when you're ready."

At the carpet, Joey passed out bowls and then sent the boxes of crackers around the circle that had formed. I sat next to Thea and tucked the trail mix between us.

As she handed me a bowl, Thea winked and said, "We got this. Don't worry."

Rosie was sitting on the other side of me, and when she started to hand over the box of crackers, Thea leaned in front of me and took it. "Pour the trail mix now," Thea whispered to me.

I took the lid off my trail mix and shook some into my bowl. My eyes darted around the circle, and then I smiled at Thea. She was right. No one noticed.

Almost no one.

"Ah-hem." Joey cleared his throat. He was standing in the middle of the circle with his hands on his hips. "Chef Blaire? Is my snack not gourmet enough for you?"

A couple of kids laughed, and my face went red-hot. Everyone was staring at me, and I didn't know what to do. It was the moment I'd feared, but a thousand times worse.

"Here, Amadi," Thea said loudly, passing the cheese crackers without taking any. Thea held her bowl out to me. "Can I have some of your trail mix?" she asked.

Before I could answer, Thea reached into the container and grabbed a dried cherry. She threw it into the air and tried to catch it in her mouth. She missed, and the cherry bounced off her nose. Everyone laughed, and Thea grinned from her spot on the carpet.

"Blaire's swapping out a snack from home," Ms. Lewis said. "Joey, thanks for these crackers. Have a seat. Let's all talk about what's coming up this week."

"Thank you," I whispered to Thea as Ms. Lewis started to talk about our science project.

"Any time," she said, popping an almond into her mouth.

After going through a short list, Ms. Lewis put her notepad aside and leaned into the circle. "The most important thing I want to talk about right now is the Fifth-Grade Community Service Challenge."

"Here it comes!" Thea whispered in my ear, nudging me.

"You're now the oldest students at Bluefield Elementary," Ms. Lewis said. "And you've grown and learned so much since you started school. The Community Service Challenge is about taking all that learning and turning it into something that helps our community."

Thea and I exchanged a thumbs-up. Bring it on!

"This goes beyond our classroom and school community," Ms. Lewis continued. "This is about our larger Bluefield community. What do you care about when it comes to our city and your neighbors? How can you contribute to something that matters to you personally?" She paused, glancing around at us.

I shook the trail mix in my bowl, mixing the different ingredients around. I always thought of the guests at the B and B, the restaurant staff, and the farm crew as my community. So much of my world was about the people at my home and the people who came through there. I'd always been able to contribute to *that* community. Now I wondered what I could do for the Bluefield community.

"Keep in mind that community service comes in different shapes and sizes," Ms. Lewis told us. "It doesn't have to be big or take up tons of time."

I stared out the window, my mind spinning. I love doing things big. Now I had a chance to make a big difference. I couldn't help but think of the display case in the hallway. How awesome would it be if one of my big ideas became a permanent part of Bluefield Elementary?

I looked at Thea and grinned. I'd never done anything like this before, but I couldn't wait to try.

*

"The animal shelter," Sabrina said as she hung upside down on the giant spiderweb on our playground at recess. "I'm going to see if my parents will let me foster kittens."

"Maybe I could help my mom coach the little kids' soccer team," Rosie said. "Ten five-year-olds plus ten soccer balls? She could definitely use an assistant."

"Some people from my Greek dance troupe perform at senior centers and hospitals," Thea said. "I should find out if I can join them."

"What about you, Blaire?" asked Rosie. "You're always good at ideas." The wind kicked up a bit, and Rosie tugged on the sleeves of her shirt, trying to pull them down. "Urgh, I told my mom this was too small! I had a growth spurt over the summer and none of my clothes fit anymore."

"Same here," Thea said. "I had to buy a bunch of new pants for school."

POP! I had a brainstorm. I called them idea-sparks when they came all of a sudden but at just the right moment.

"Hey!" I said. "My brother and I have a ton of stuff we've outgrown, too. I could collect all the clothing my family doesn't need anymore and give it away. My mom always brings things to the Bluefield Helping Hands Center."

"Make sure the clothes are in season," said an unfamiliar voice. "No one's looking for summer stuff right now."

We all spun around. The new kid, Eli, was sitting in the wood chips underneath the slide, with a tablet on his lap.

"Hey!" Amadi said, dropping down from the spiderweb. "We're not allowed to have devices at school."

Eli turned his tablet off but didn't say anything else. I hopped down from the spiderweb.

Grandpa always says, *It only takes one kind word to make someone feel welcome.* That was his motto at the B and B.

"That's good advice," I said. "Thanks."

Eli looked up for only a second, then back down.

"I'm Blaire. This is Sabrina, Amadi, Rose, and Thea."

"Okay," he mumbled.

"I like your T-shirt," I continued.

"My dad has socks with taco dinosaurs," Thea added. "You know. Tacosaurus."

I saw a quick smile cross Eli's face, but he didn't say anything.

"Maybe no one explained the rules about devices," I continued. "They're not allowed."

He just shrugged and replied, "Ms. Cheeger explained all the rules." Then he got up, tucked the tablet under his shirt, and walked away.

"All righty then," Rose said.

"*That* was awkward," Thea added.

"He could be, you know, a little friendlier," Sabrina said.

"He's probably nervous with the new school thing," I said. "I'm sure he'll warm up."

"I hope you're right," Thea said.

As I watched Eli walk across the playground, I wondered what friends he'd left behind when he moved. "It's going to be weird for him to pick a community service project, since he just moved here," I said.

"I didn't think of that," Sabrina said.

"Maybe we can help him," I suggested.

Thea looped her arm in mine. "Blaire, if you were a superhero, your name would be Mighty People Person."

I looked back at Eli, who was all alone. "Well, everyone could use a friend," I said. *And if Eli will let me*, I thought, *I'll be his.*

CHAPTER 4

Helping Hands

There were three items left on my bed. A green velvet dress I got for Christmas two years ago. The jeans with the embroidered flowers running down one leg that I wore every single day in third grade. A pair of old rain boots, covered in smiling ladybugs, that hadn't fit since I was five.

I loved these clothes! I'd totally outgrown them, but it was hard to put them in the giant plastic bag with the other stuff I was donating. So I'd come up with a way to "keep" them forever.

"Smile," I said as I held my tablet over the dress and took a photo. I did the same thing with the jeans and the rain boots. I was going to put the photos on the big bulletin board in my room—my inspiration board—so I'd be reminded of how great these clothes had made me feel.

As I added the clothes to one of the bags, I told them, "It's someone else's turn to love you guys now."

Mom peeked her head into my bedroom. "Ready?"

"Yup," I said, showing her my two bags of clothing and shoes. Mom, Dad, Beckett, Grandpa, and I had all gone through our closets and drawers. We had a total of eight big bags to donate!

"Awesome. Dad and Grandpa are dealing with an overflowing toilet in one of the guest rooms, so we need to get back in time to set up the afternoon coffee service."

"Yuck," I said as Mom and I each took a bag and started down the two flights of stairs. "Wait—I hope it's not Marco's room."

"That would not be *super-bonita*, would it?" Mom said from behind me.

We were on the back stairs that led to our family kitchen. I squeezed through the narrow kitchen doorway with my bulky bag. I couldn't see where I was going as I headed down the hall, so *BAM*.

I walked into something.

"Ow!"

Oh no, I walked into some*one*. Ergh, I hoped it wasn't one of our guests. I peered cautiously around the bag.

It was Cat! She was rubbing her nose from where I bonked her with the bag, her new wedding ring sparkling in the afternoon light. When she saw me, she broke into a bright smile. "Where are you going, Santa?" she joked.

"You're back!" I dropped the bag and threw my arms around her. She'd been gone for two weeks, but it had felt like two months. Pleasant View Farm just wasn't the same without her. Behind me, Mom saw Cat and dropped her bag to join us in a group hug.

"How was your honeymoon?" Mom asked when the three of us pulled apart.

"It was amazing. We hiked—"

The phone down the hall at the front desk started ringing.

"Hold that thought," Mom said, dashing to the desk.

"What's all this?" Cat asked, gesturing at the bags.

"We're donating clothes to the Helping Hands Center."

"Uh, Blaire," Mom called, her hand over the phone. "We'll have to wait and do our delivery later. I need to deal with this."

"I can take Blaire," Cat suggested. "We have a lot of

catching up to do." She raised an eyebrow at me and smiled. "I know you've got a ton to tell me."

"Thanks!" Mom said, turning back to the phone.

We took the bags to Cat's truck and loaded them into the back.

"Well, that's interesting," Cat said, nodding her head toward the herb garden, where someone was sitting in the dirt among the plants.

"Hi, Marco," I called.

Marco waved back.

"He knows there are lawn chairs, right?" Cat asked.

I giggled. "He likes to find unique spots to sit and think. He says different perspectives are good for creativity."

"Man, I missed this place," Cat murmured.

※

Cat hadn't even pulled out of the driveway when I burst out with the big news. "We saw the review in *Empire State Weddings*!"

"No way," Cat said. "Is it—"

"—it's amazing."

"Oh my gosh," Cat said, suddenly nervous. "We haven't even seen pictures from our wedding photographer. Does everything look okay?"

"*Okay?* It looks incredible! When we get back, Marco will show you the magazine and you can see for yourself."

"Marco? As in, the guy in the herb garden?"

"As in Marco Gonzalez from *Room Revolutions*!"

"That design show you and your mom watch? Cool," Cat said with a smile. "And he's staying at the B and B?"

"Yup," I said. "He came to Pleasant View Farm because of your wedding review."

Cat shook her head. "He came to Pleasant View Farm because it's a special place."

I nodded. "Marco said it was magical."

"Marco's right about that," Cat said, pulling into the driveway for Bluefield Helping Hands. It was a small brick building with a parking lot full of cars.

"There's the donation bin over there," I said, pointing to a giant metal yellow box in the corner of the parking lot. But when we pulled closer to it, I saw a sign taped near the top:

OUR BIN DOOR IS BROKEN. PLEASE BRING DONATIONS INSIDE!

We parked and took a load inside. Even though I'd driven by Helping Hands, I'd never gone inside. One wall was covered in a cool mural of a rainbow with a group of people underneath—they were all sizes and colors. Over by another wall, a woman was hanging something on a bulletin board.

"Clothing donations?" she asked when she saw us with our plastic bags.

"Yup," Cat said. "Blaire here collected items from her whole family. We've got more to bring in."

The woman smiled at me. "Thank you! This is perfect timing, because we have some volunteers coming today to sort through clothes. I'm Eileen. Let me help you with the other bags."

Eileen got a cart and helped load the rest of the bags. Then she brought us down a hallway to a room filled with empty plastic bins, all labeled with signs like GIRLS SIZES 7–9 and BOYS, INFANT SIZES. There were other bags and boxes of donated clothing, and we put ours in the pile with them.

"This is a busy time for us," Eileen explained. "Folks are coming in to get new clothes for school and warmer clothes for the winter."

I glanced at Cat. Mom always takes Beckett and me to the mall to get whatever new clothes we need. *This is what some families have to do instead*, I thought.

As we walked back toward the lobby, we passed an open doorway to a room that looked a lot like our restaurant storeroom. There were tall shelves filled with boxes and cans of food, and some people setting up grocery bags on a table.

"That's our food pantry," Eileen explained. "Our Saturday distribution hours are about to start. We're always looking for donations for that, too."

"Blaire? Blaire!" I heard a small voice and turned around. "It's you! You're Blaire!"

A young girl and a man were walking toward us. She looked familiar, but I couldn't think of her name.

"I'm Abby," she said. "I was in Beckett's first-grade class last year? I remember you from his birthday party."

"Oh, hi!" I said to them both, realizing the man was Abby's dad. "What's up?"

"Nothing much," Abby said, shrugging. She was holding a pencil and a pad of paper with some doodles on it. "Getting some help with our groceries because we're having a hard time right now."

"Abby . . ." her dad said, and cleared his throat. "You don't need to tell people that."

"Why not?" she asked. "You said it was no big deal and I shouldn't be embarrassed."

"That's absolutely right," Eileen said, reaching out to muss Abby's hair. "We're happy we can be here when families need us. There's lots of good stuff in there today, Abby. We just got a donation of apples and lettuce greens from a local farm."

Cat perked up at that. "You know," she said to Eileen. "We're from Pleasant View Farm. I'll talk to Blaire's folks about arranging a produce donation."

"Oh, wow," Eileen said, turning to me. "I read the food blog that you and your mom write. Her restaurant is one of my favorite places in Bluefield. It's a real gem in our community."

"Thanks," I said. "I'll tell my mom."

"And I'll let you know about the donation," Cat added.

"Wonderful," Eileen said, handing Cat a pamphlet with the center's number on it. "We can never have enough fresh food to offer our families. It all goes so quickly."

"We've learned to get in line early," Abby's dad said.

"That's why I bring my drawing stuff, because it's boring to wait," Abby added. "But it's okay if we don't get the green things. I hate those!"

"*Abby*," her dad said, shaking his head. Then he turned to me. "We can't get her to eat any vegetables. We've tried cooking them lots of different ways, but she always turns her nose up."

"Once, when I was little," Abby added, "I threw some spinach across the room because it tasted so gross! There's still a stain on the wall!"

I knew everyone had vegetables they didn't like, but I couldn't imagine not eating—or cooking—any at all.

Suddenly: *idea-spark!* "Hey, Abby," I said. "Have you ever tried cooking vegetables yourself?"

"*Ewww,* no," she replied, scrunching up her nose. "Plus, I'm only seven. I don't cook."

"But anyone can cook, especially if you have a grown-up's help. I cook all the time! Do you remember the lunch from Beckett's birthday party? I made that with my mom."

Abby's eyes grew wide. "Those were the best chicken tenders ever. And Beckett had a very delicious cake, too."

"What if I gave you some of my favorite vegetable recipes?" I asked. "Would you try one?"

Abby gave me a sideways look, then smiled. "If I do, will you make lunch for *my* birthday in October—including cake?"

Her dad started to say something, but I held out my hand to Abby for a high five.

"Deal!" I said as Abby slapped my palm. "But back to those veggies—I'll make up some recipe cards and you can pick one."

"That's a great idea," Eileen said, her eyes bright with excitement. "Would you be able to make extra? I'd love to have some available here at the center for other kids and their parents to take."

"Of course," I said. "I'll make a whole bunch."

"Dad!" Abby burst out suddenly, tugging her dad down the hall. "The pantry's open."

"Bye, Abby!" I called.

"Bye, Blaire! Can't wait for my birthday lunch!" Abby suddenly rushed back to me and handed me a piece of paper. "Here. I drew this puppy wearing a fairy costume. You can have it."

"Thanks," I said, taking the drawing. I couldn't

help but smile. Goats in pj's. Puppies in fairy costumes. Abby and I had a lot in common.

"I should go help with the distribution," Eileen said, waving to me and Cat as she started to follow them. "We'll talk soon, I'm sure!"

As Cat and I walked out of the building, past other families who were arriving for the food distribution hours, Cat put her arm around me.

"I'm glad that donation bin was broken," she said.

"Why?" I asked.

"Well, it's one thing to push a bag of clothes through a little door. It's much cooler to meet the people who Helping Hands actually helps."

I carefully folded the drawing Abby gave me and tucked it into my pocket. Cat was right. The center wasn't a place for random strangers anymore. It was there for a kid I knew. And I could do something to help her.

I couldn't wait to get started on my recipe cards.

CHAPTER 5

Inspiration in the Attic

Wooooo. Woooo."

"Thea, stop making ghost noises!" I nudged my friend as we sat in the back seat of Grandpa's van the next day. "You're creeping me out!"

"This *place* is creeping me out," Thea replied.

We were heading up a narrow, winding road lined with droopy willow trees on either side. The branches swayed in the breeze and looked like arms that were trying to grab the van. The driveway was full of potholes, and even though Grandpa was going slowly, we were getting bumped and jostled around. A thick morning mist made it impossible to see what was ahead of us.

We rounded a sharp bend and suddenly there it was, four stories high. I'd seen stone houses before—they were all over the Hudson Valley—but never one this big. Or this eerie. Several windows were boarded shut and scraggly vines hung over the porch. Two of the front steps were broken.

"Haunted," Thea whispered. "Definitely."

"Empty," Grandpa said with a chuckle. "For years." He parked the van behind three other cars in the driveway, and I recognized Marco's motorcycle. "A family who just moved to Bluefield is fixing it up."

"It's going to take a loooooooot of fixing," Thea said.

I nodded. "What a fun project. I can't wait to see the inside."

Grandpa knocked on the ginormous front door.

"I bet this thing is going to open by itself," Thea whispered as I rolled my eyes at her. When the door did open, I was grateful someone was standing behind it.

"You must be the Pleasant View Farm folks!" the woman said. "I'm—"

"—Suzanne!" I interrupted. "Marco's assistant. I recognize you from the videos. I'm Blaire, this is my friend Thea, and my grandpa Ben."

"Come on in." Suzanne smiled as she led us inside. "Marco's hard at work in the library."

Suzanne walked us through the house, which was dim and dusty but full of ornate woodwork. "Look at those molded ceilings," Grandpa said, and I craned my neck to see swans flying along the rooms. There was a wide staircase with a wooden banister. There were posts with enormous swans carved into them on either side.

Thea paused to copy the swan's pose, stretching her neck long and spreading her hands like wings. I giggled and tugged her down the hallway.

The library was a big space with tall windows and built-in bookcases. There were bright lights set up around the room. Marco was perched on a ladder in front of an enormous fireplace. Behind him was a man with a video camera and a woman with a fuzzy black microphone attached to the end of a long pole.

"Blaire! Thea!" Marco called when he saw us. "Welcome. Hello, Mr. O'Connell. You girls are here at just the right moment. I need someone with small fingers!"

Thea and I exchanged a confused look. *Strange, but interesting.*

When we got closer I saw that Marco was creating an intricate mosaic on the wall above the antique wooden fireplace mantel. Colorful tile mosaics were one of his specialties since they were a big part of traditional Mexican culture.

Marco had finished one corner, with tiles of different shapes and sizes that were a pretty blue-green color. There was a sun design drawn in pencil in the center of the wall, and a box of yellow tiles nearby.

"I have some teeny-tiny tiles I'd like to squeeze in," Marco said, pointing. "Right there. Can you do it for me? My fingers are too thick."

"Really?" I said. "We get to help?"

Thea and I each took turns adding tile pieces to the mosaic with special glue. At first, Marco showed us where to put the tiles, but then he let us decide. It was like doing a jigsaw puzzle, except more fun, because where you put one piece determined where the next one would go.

Marco's videos always showed him making his mosaics in fast motion, but seeing the real thing in real-time motion was amazing. After half an hour, Thea and I had added dozens of tiles, but the mosaic still had a long way to go.

"I never knew it took so much time to do this," Thea said.

"Me either," I agreed. "And it's so cool to see them up close and then step back and get a whole different image."

"Perspective!" Marco said. "It's magical to look at the same thing from different points of view."

"That's why you sit in the dirt, right?" I asked.

Marco's crew laughed. Thea looked confused.

"Well, you girls did a great job on the mosaic. *Fabuloso!*" he announced. "I've had a sketch of this sun design in my notebook for months, and I was just waiting for the right wall to come along. I walked in here and realized, of course! It needs to go above a fireplace! Fire, flame, sun!"

"Wow," I said. "I have an inspiration board in my room where I keep ideas for projects."

Marco smiled. "Something small can become something big, no?"

All I could do was nod. It was crazy and wonderful to be talking about this stuff with a professional designer. "Are you doing 'room revolutions' on the whole house?" I asked.

"Most of it. The Masons—that's the family who bought this place—knew it needed a lot of work, but they fell in love with it. And I did, too. We'll redesign the entire downstairs and a few of the second-floor bedrooms."

"Which room does the ghost live in?" Thea asked, making her creepy *Wooooo* noise again.

"It does seem like that kind of house," Marco said with a laugh. "So far we haven't seen anything spooky, but go ahead and explore the house! Let us know what you discover."

Suzanne appeared, and Marco called, "Paperwork break." The guy with the camera stopped filming. Funny, I'd forgotten he was there.

When Grandpa started chatting with the crew, Thea looked at me and stroked an imaginary beard. It was something she did as part of her "evil villain" character.

"So . . ." Thea said, sounding super devious. "Where should we start our snooping? Upstairs?"

"Oh yeah," I said. "Race you."

I took off up the staircase, Thea behind me. We stopped short on the second-floor landing. There was a long hall lined with doors. All the doors were open, and dust motes floated in the dim light. *Creepy.*

"Let's go all the way up," Thea said. "Ghosts love attics."

We climbed another flight of stairs and found

another long hallway. It was darker, and creepier, up here. All the doors were closed.

"This is my kind of spooky," Thea said, then put her hand on the first door's knob. "Okay, what do you think is in here?"

"Hmmmm," I said. "Probably a bedroom."

It was an empty closet. We made our way down the hall, making crazy guesses about what was behind each door. *A bathroom big enough for an elephant to take a shower. A kid's bedroom filled with stuffed animals.* Of course we were wrong every time. The rooms were all empty and dark.

"Now this one," Thea said, reaching for the handle of a narrow door at the end of the hallway, "is a portal to a secret universe where pigs fly and . . . everyone's purple."

"Okay, then," I said, laughing. "Let's go!"

I flung open the door, expecting to see another closet.

WHOA.

"*Stairs!*" Thea exclaimed. "Steps to a secret universe! Told you!"

"Or to the ghost's bedroom," I said. The stairs were

narrow, even narrower than the back stairway at my house, and they didn't look all that sturdy.

"Come on," Thea said as she started climbing the stairs.

"Maybe we should go up with an adult . . ." I said, but Thea was already halfway up.

When we reached the top of the stairs, Thea flicked a light switch in the wall.

WHOA again.

It was a giant attic space, stretching as far as we could see—it must have gone the length of the whole house. The wooden beams of the arching roof reminded me of a cathedral we visited in the city once. Thea and I took a few steps. The floors creaked under our feet.

"Gah!" Thea exclaimed as she walked right into a spiderweb.

"Ew," I said, wiping the web from her face and flicking it off my fingers.

"I'm okay," Thea said, distracted. She walked into the middle of the space and turned slowly in a circle. "If this were my house, I'd turn this into the Theodora Theater. I'd build a stage down at that end, with seats over here." Thea motioned with her arms to show me where her audience would be. "Then we'd have a place to perform our own plays and stuff! What about you?"

"I'd turn this into a playroom . . ." I looked up at the wooden beams. *BAM*. Idea-spark! "Wait, not just a playroom. A play*ground*. With swings and everything!"

"*Super-bonita!*" a voice boomed behind us.

Thea and I screamed.

It was just Marco, but my heart was pounding. "I had no idea you were there," I stammered.

"Sorry," Marco said with a laugh as the rest of the crew followed him up into the attic. "But what else would be in this attic playground of yours, Blaire?" he asked.

"What else?" I asked, starting to walk around, getting a feel for the space and my idea-spark. "Well, it's tall enough for a fort with different levels. And a climbing wall. And slides—that land in a huge ball pit." I looked up at the beams. "You could hang swings from the rafters, and some rope ladders, too. And there's plenty of space for a seesaw."

Marco retraced my loop around the attic, followed by his crew. He was smiling. "I'm seeing what you're seeing," he said. "What would you put on the walls?"

"That side could be painted blue with white clouds, like a sky," I said, then pointed to the other wall. "And that one could be painted dark blue with stars, like night."

"Yes! I see that, too! Ah, this will be a fantastic surprise for the Masons."

"Wait—you're really going to turn this attic into an indoor playground?" I asked in disbelief.

"Of course!" Marco said. "It's too good of an idea. The family has four kids. They would love it, and it would be a true room revolution, no? Suzanne! Come, come, let's capture this inspiration into notes."

Suzanne rushed over to Marco and they started talking, the camera crew circling them.

Thea stepped up beside me and took my hand, squeezing it. "A-mazing," she said.

BAM. Idea-spark number three.

"Hey, Marco?" I said. "Thea had a great idea. There should be a stage and seats at one end. The kids can act out skits and put on plays."

"*Fantastico!*" Marco exclaimed.

Thea's eyes grew wide. She squeezed my hand even tighter. Our ideas were going to be on *Room Revolutions*!

"This is SO much better than finding a ghost," she whispered.

꙳꙳꙳

When I got home, Beckett was in the pen with Dash and Penny. He was wearing his magic hat and holding my old Hula-Hoop.

"How's the goat act coming along?" I asked.

"Great," Beckett answered. "Now I'm teaching Dash how to jump through a hoop."

Behind Beckett, Dash was chewing on the hoop.

"Good luck," I called, heading inside.

I found Mom and Dad in the Pleasant View Farm office.

"We don't even have a calendar for 2021 yet!" Dad was saying as I peeked my head in. He and Mom were sitting at a round table, with papers spread out in front of them.

"Well, we'd better get one," Mom replied. "People plan weddings really far in advance. Hi, honey."

"How was the house Marco's working on?" Dad asked.

"It was *amazing*." I sat down and told them everything, from the spooky driveway to the attic adventure and my idea for the playground. "And Marco says he's going to do it!"

Mom was impressed. "That all sounds pretty exciting."

"Here's the best part," I said. "He filmed me telling him my ideas, and he wants to put it in the show. But he needs your permission first."

Mom and Dad exchanged a glance, and Dad said, "Okay. We'll talk to Marco when he comes back."

"*Fantastico!*" I said. Then I jumped up. "I'll be upstairs. I have to watch some *Room Revolutions* episodes for more inspiration. See you later."

"Hold up there, TV star."

I turned back.

"You seem to be forgetting something," Mom said, tapping her watch. "It's called Chore Revolution. Visiting Marco's set doesn't get you out of that."

"Ah, right," I said. I looked at the papers on the table and saw that they were calendar pages. "What's going on here?"

"*Empire State Weddings* hit the stands yesterday,"

Dad explained. "We've gotten over thirty emails from people interested in booking the Barn at Pleasant View Farm. Not to mention about fifty phone calls."

The phone out on the front desk began to ring.

"Make that fifty-one," Mom said. "Marco was right. We're about to get busier than we've ever been before. We've already booked every weekend through the end of the year."

That was great news. "I can fill in at the front desk whenever you need," I chimed in. "And I'm always ready to help with more event designs . . ."

"Nice try," Mom said. "But remember—school comes first."

"I know. But I'll have time on the weekends."

"Blaire, I know you're not happy unless you're creating or organizing or designing something," Dad said, getting up and putting his arm around me. "But don't take on more than you can manage."

"I won't," I said.

"Well, you won't *mean* to," Mom added.

"Okaaaay." I sighed. "I get it."

"Good," Dad said, kissing the top of my head. "End of lecture. Off to your chores."

CHAPTER 6

It's Just Pizza

I held the box in my lap, flipping through my newly created recipe cards as Dad drove me and Beckett to school. "Tell me what you ended up with," Dad said.

I pulled the first card out and read it. "Forest Giant Fingers."

"Oven-fried green beans," Dad said. "Right?"

"Right," I answered. "It's the best way to eat a green bean."

Dad nodded. "Next?"

"Maple-Bacon Roasted Carrots."

Dad smacked his lips. "Mmmmm . . . maple-bacon anything sounds delicious."

"Definitely! Next is Spinach and Potato Stars," I said.

"Those are even better when they're shaped like bugs," Beckett offered from the back seat.

"I'll make a note of that," I said. Then I looked at Dad and shook my head.

I flipped to the next card. "Veggie Rainbow Kabobs with Cloud Sauce."

"Cloud sauce?" Dad asked.

"Ranch dressing," I answered.

"With a clever name!" Dad said.

I pulled out the last card. "And finally, Broccoli Cheddar Hug-in-a-Bowl."

"Why don't you just call it soup?" Beckett asked.

"Because this is the ultimate comfort food, and it's too comforting to just call it soup," I explained.

"But you can't even eat that anymore," Beckett said. "Or the ranch dressing."

I turned to look at Beckett in the back seat. "No, but these are my all-time favorites," I said. "I'm pretty sure Abby and the other kids will like them." I turned around and looked at Dad. "Maybe Mom would help me experiment with a nondairy version of the cheddar soup."

Dad reached over and squeezed my shoulder. "I'm sure she would. I'm proud of you, honey. You've done a great job learning to cook—and eat—without dairy."

"Thanks." I sighed. I wanted to tell Dad that it was still kinda hard. Especially at school. But Beckett was leaning forward, peering into the shoebox in my lap.

"How many of those cards are in there?" he asked.

"I made five copies of each recipe. Hopefully, twenty-five kids like Abby will try them."

"We'll know soon enough," Dad said, pulling into the Helping Hands parking lot.

I'd wanted to drop the cards off today, before the food pantry distribution hours tomorrow. That way, kids could take the cards home when they came to get groceries for the week. Dad pulled up in front of the entrance, and I hopped out. Eileen met me outside the front door.

"Wowza, Blaire," she said as I handed her the box. I'd covered it with green paper and drawn vines and vegetables all over it so it looked like a garden. On the top of the box, I'd written, HEY, KIDS! COOK UP SOME FUN WITH FRESH VEGGIES! "Thank you so much!" Eileen added. "Abby and the other kids are going to love this!"

"I hope so," I said, climbing back into the car.

As we headed for school, I asked Dad if he thought the recipe cards should be my official project for the Community Service Challenge. "I'm supposed to find something that's important and interesting to me," I explained.

"Well, this does seem to fit the bill," Dad said.

"True, but I'm not sure it's big enough."

Dad smiled. "Well, I guess it depends on what you mean by 'big,'" he said. "You went to the center to donate clothes, and ended up creating these recipe cards. Cat went to the center with you and *she* ended up arranging for Pleasant View Farm to donate produce to the pantry every week. So you started a chain reaction of helping. That seems big to me."

I thought about what Marco had said at the Mason house. "Something small can become something big."

Would this little box of cards become something big enough for my Community Service Challenge project?

"Okay, my friends!" Ms. Lewis called. "Line up for lunch!"

It was the first Pizza Friday of the year, and I'd been dreading it ever since the first Monday Madness snack episode. I had to eat something different, and this time I'd be in the cafeteria, in front of the whole school.

"Maybe Ms. Lewis would let me eat in the classroom," I said to Thea. "Or I could go to the nurse's office."

"Nope," Thea said matter-of-factly. "There's just going to be another Pizza Friday next month, and then another and another. Better to get this over with."

I went to my cubby and grabbed my lunch box. I knew I'd be the only one who had brought lunch from home. *Everybody* got pizza on Friday. It was the best day of the month. Or used to be.

It's still Pizza Friday, I told myself as I walked down the hall with my friends. *Just a new version for me.*

Since I didn't have to go through the cafeteria food line, I was the first one of my friends to sit down at our usual table, third on the right next to the window. I started unpacking my lunch box.

Sabrina plopped her tray onto the table and slid into the seat across from me. The pizza on her plate smelled so, so good. I tried not to look at it as I opened the container I'd brought.

"What's in there?" Sabrina asked.

"My own personal dairy-free pizza," I replied. "Mom and I made the crust last night and baked it this morning. She packed it so it would stay warm."

We'd done some experimenting and found a kind of soy cheese that tasted melty-gooey good. The sauce was made with tomatoes we'd grown on the farm. The pepperoni was from one of the meat suppliers we used for the restaurant.

"Anything you and your mom make is amazing," Sabrina said.

"Your mini-pizza is adorable!" Amadi said as she sank down next to me.

"I wish *our* pizza had pepperoni on it," Rosie added as she settled into her seat.

I took a bite of my little pizza just as two girls from another class walked past our table.

"Since when do you bring your own pizza on Fridays, Blaire?" one of them asked.

I blushed a deep red. Just like on Mondays, it felt like the room was suddenly quiet and everyone was staring at me.

Thea slammed her tray down next to me and crossed her arms in front of her chest. "Blaire brings her own pizza. Is that a problem?" She took a step toward the girls, and they hurried away, looking sorry they asked.

I started laughing. "Thanks, cafeteria guard dog," I told Thea as she sat down.

"*Woof, woof.* Anytime," Thea said with a grin. "I mean, seriously, it's just pizza. And it's not like you're the only one with food stuff to deal with." She pointed over at the Nut-Free Table, where kids who had nut allergies sat to make sure they weren't exposed to anything that could make them sick.

"You're right," I said. "Being around other people eating dairy isn't dangerous for me." I was glad I didn't have to sit at a separate table, without my friends. There were plenty of people who had it worse than me in the Foods You Can't Eat department. Some kids could get really sick, like rush-to-the-hospital sick, if they accidentally ate something with nuts in it. If *I* ate dairy, I'd get some pretty bad stomach cramps, but that wasn't the same thing.

Eli walked past our table, holding his tray, scanning the room for a place to sit. He found an empty table in the corner and sat down by himself.

"He's done that every day this week," Amadi whispered. "It's like he doesn't even want to try to make friends."

"We should invite him to sit with us," I suggested, climbing out of my seat.

"That's nice of you, Blaire!" Rose said.

"Mighty People Person to the rescue!" Thea added.

I noticed that Eli's T-shirt said GUESS WHAT? with a picture of a chicken and an arrow pointing to its rear end. It took me a second to figure it out: Guess what, chicken butt? I giggled. Eli had a good sense of humor in there somewhere.

"Hey," I said, with a little wave.

"Mmmmm," Eli replied, chewing his pizza. Then he swallowed and said, "What's up?"

"Do you want to come sit with us?"

Eli peered over at our table, where my friends were pretending *not* to look at him, even though it was totally obvious they were looking at him. "No, thanks. I'm good."

"Okay. Then can I sit here for a minute?"

Eli just shrugged. I sat down.

"So what do you think of Bluefield so far?" I asked.

"Haven't seen much yet," he mumbled, looking up at me for only a second, then back down at his pizza. "My mom and I have been busy unpacking. But . . . mountains, yeah. Lots of woods and farms, cool."

I sat up straighter. "*I* live on a farm. My family owns Pleasant View Farm. Have you heard of it?"

Eli shook his head.

"We'll have a booth at the Bluefield Harvest Festival tomorrow. You should come visit us there. There's food, crafts, music, and a farmers' market. They close off Main Street, and the library runs a used book sale. There's even a bounce house and pony rides."

"Pony rides?" Eli said.

"Okay, maybe that's not your style," I said with a laugh. "But the bicycle shop has a booth right by the Rail Trail, and you can get your bike tuned up for free. The festival's a great way to check out all the different things to do around here."

"Bluefield Harvest Festival," Eli said. "Got it."

He started eating again, and I kept talking.

"We'll have some of our produce for sale," I added. "We grow food on the farm, and my mom's the chef at our restaurant. My grandpa runs a bed-and-breakfast in our house. And my dad just renovated an old barn for big events like weddings. I helped. We have chickens and a goat and a lamb. I just made them pajamas."

He raised an eyebrow. "Pajamas?"

"You kind of have to see it to get how awesome it was. If you go to the blog on our farm website, there's a video."

Now Eli put down his pizza, and his eyes looked bright and excited. "You make videos?"

"Sometimes. Why?"

"I make them, too. Like, all the time. I started making them with my—"

Eli stopped and looked at someone behind me. It was Thea.

"Hi, guys. Can I join you?"

"Um, I'm done," Eli said. He stood up, shoving the last of his pizza in his mouth, then grabbed his tray and left without another word.

"Sorry," Thea said to me. "It looked like you guys were actually talking, so I came over to say hi."

"We were talking," I said. "He likes to make videos with . . . well, that's all I know." I shrugged.

Thea smiled. "Hey, you found out something about the mysterious Eli! Leave it to Blaire. Want to get a Popsicle?" she asked.

"For sure." Thea and I were both allowed to get desserts on Fridays. Mom and I had talked about the snacks

I could buy, and fruit Popsicles were totally safe for me to eat.

As we joined the others at the ice cream freezer, Thea and I both grabbed a strawberry Popsicle.

"I declare," Thea said dramatically, waving her Popsicle like a wand, "that 'Pizza Friday' is to be hereby known as '*Popsicle* Friday.'"

"Deal," I said, and we touched our Popsicles together.

I looked back to see Eli heading out the door to recess. He'd seemed so excited when we were talking about videos. What was he going to say before Thea came over?

CHAPTER 7

A Party for Our Whole Town

6:01 a.m.

Thea: *Blaire? BLAIRE! Are you up? WAKE UP, SLEEPYHEAD!* ⏰

6:14 a.m.

Thea: *OMG, I can't believe you're not up yet. Call me!* 📞📞📞

6:27 a.m.

Amadi: *I just saw it! Blaire, you were great! Sabrina, did you watch yet?*

Sabrina: *Yeah! Blaire, can I get your autograph?*

HUH?

I wiped the sleep from my eyes and replied to the messages by typing a "speak no evil" monkey-face emoji. Thea and I had decided a few weeks ago that we'd send the monkey whenever we didn't understand what someone was trying to say in a text conversation. Now all our friends were using it.

Blaire: 🙊

Thea: *YOU DON'T KNOW?????* 😮

Sabrina: *OMG she doesn't know.*

Amadi: *WATCH THIS!*

The next message to come through was a link to an online video. I clicked on it . . . and it opened up the *Room Revolutions* channel.

No. Way.

There was Marco, showing the audience the attic in the stone mansion. Next came a girl talking about how she would turn that space into an indoor playground. And that girl was *me*. Thea was in the video, too.

Then Marco and Suzanne talked about how they could take "their friend Blaire's" great ideas and make them a reality.

There were a few scenes with Marco, Suzanne, and a construction crew building the play structure I'd talked about. It was all there. They sped up the tape so it looked like everyone was working really fast, and it was hilarious.

Finally, it was my favorite part of all of Marco's videos: the moment the home's owners saw the "after" part of the room makeover. Marco brought the couple and their kids—a nine-year-old boy, a six-year-old girl, and twin toddlers—up the attic stairs and had them cover their eyes. When they opened them, they all gasped and laughed. The kids rushed toward the play structure, and the parents hugged Marco.

When the video was over, I scrolled down the page to see that it already had thousands of likes and hundreds of comments. Whoa!

I jumped out of bed and ran down the two flights of stairs to the front desk, where Dad was eating a breakfast wrap with one hand and trying to type with the other.

"Did you see this?" I asked, waving my tablet at him.

"What did Beckett do to your tablet *now*?" Dad said, sighing.

"No! The video! Marco's video!"

Dad just blinked at me, blankly. "What video?"

"Daaaad!"

Dad dropped his act now, breaking into a wide smile. "Yes, of course I saw it. Marco showed it to me and Mom yesterday. He wanted us to see it before he posted it, to make sure the part with you in it looked okay."

"And you didn't tell me?"

He shrugged. "We figured it would be more fun for you to find out from your friends. They must be excited."

"Uh . . . just a little," I said, handing Dad my tablet and showing him the string of messages.

"There she is!" said a voice above me. "*Room Revolutions'* newest design consultant."

I looked up to see Marco coming down the stairs. "Tell me you watched it," he added when he reached the first floor.

"I watched it."

"Did you love, love, love it?"

"It's so cool, Marco! I wish I could have been there when you did the big reveal."

"Me too! We'll have you there for the big moment next time."

Next time? "Uh . . . sure!"

Cat came in the front door. "Hey, Sprout, you're still in your pajamas? I've got the truck loaded up. We've got to go get set up for the festival."

I grabbed my tablet from Dad and handed it to Cat. "I'll go get dressed, but first, you *have* to watch this!"

✳

Cat loved the video, and I watched it over and over as she drove into town. As Cat and I finished setting up our booth, Thea arrived.

"Small fingers!" Thea shouted when she saw me. We watched the video together three more times. We would have kept going, but when Mom showed up, she said we had to shut off the tablet. "Go enjoy the festival," she said, unpacking supplies for samples from the restaurant menu.

Thea and I were leaving the booth when I felt something tugging at the back of my T-shirt. I turned to see Abby and her dad.

"Abby insisted on coming to the Pleasant View Farm booth first," Abby's dad explained. "She wanted to see you."

Abby smiled and pulled a piece of paper out of her pocket, then handed it to me. It was another drawing, this one of a heart with arms and legs and a face saying, THANK YOU FOR THE RECIPES, BLAIRE! in a speech bubble.

"I love it," I said, clutching the drawing to my chest. "Which recipe did you take?"

"I took two of them: the one with the giant fingers, and the one with the soup."

"How did they turn out?" I asked.

"The fingers came out good. They were yummy!"

Abby's dad smiled and flashed me a thumbs-up.

"That's Beckett's favorite, too," I told her. "What about the Hug-in-a-Bowl?"

"We couldn't make that one." Abby scrunched up her face. "They didn't have broccoli at Helping Hands this week."

"Hopefully next time," her dad added.

"Oh, right," I said, puzzling out what Abby and her dad were saying. They couldn't always get the ingredients they need for a recipe. At my house, all I have to do is walk outside to get fresh vegetables. My friends' families can just buy what they need at the supermarket. *But some people can't do either*, I realized.

Abby shrugged it off, though. "Will you go with me into the bounce house?"

"Yeah, of course!" I said. "This is my friend Thea. Can she come, too?"

"Sure."

Ten minutes later, Abby, Thea, and I were having a contest to see how many times we could jump high enough to touch the roof of the bounce house. Thea tried to do some of her moves from her Greek dance troupe, and I showed Abby how to do a seat drop.

After our time in the bounce house was up, we tumbled out, one after the other, our faces red from laughing so much. Abby's dad was waiting for her.

"Hey, we're going to grab some kettle corn. Want to come?" I asked Abby.

Abby looked hopefully at her dad, but he bit his lip and shook his head. "Maybe another time," he said. "We'd better get going."

Thea and I said good-bye to them and headed for the kettle corn booth. I looked back as we walked, and noticed that Abby and her dad *weren't* leaving. They were at the library book sale, looking through the bin marked ONE FREE BOOK FOR EVERY CHILD!

Then I got it: Abby's dad probably said no because they didn't have the money to buy kettle corn. It probably wasn't easy for him to explain that. I thought about how difficult it was for me to explain why I couldn't eat dairy. I guess I knew how Abby's dad felt.

I wanted to run after Abby and tell her I'd use all my saved-up allowance to buy her as much kettle corn as she wanted, but when I looked back again, she and her dad were gone.

I spotted a booth with the Bluefield Helping Hands banner. Eileen was at the table, handing out fliers and free magnets with the center's information on it.

"Hi, Blaire!" Eileen said when Thea and I came up to the table. "Your recipe cards were a hit! Lots of kids took them. We could use more, if you're up for making them."

"Yeah, sure," I said. "But I hope kids can actually make the recipes. I didn't realize that some people couldn't get all the ingredients."

"It's true," Eileen said. "I suppose we could offer only the recipes that match the produce we have that week, but I'm never sure what we're going to get, and when." Now she sighed. "There are so many families dealing with food insecurity right now, and they depend on us."

"What's food insecurity?" Thea asked.

"It's when you don't have regular access to nutritious food," Eileen explained. "Some families don't know, from day to day, what they'll be able to feed their kids."

"Oh my gosh," Thea said. "That's awful. How does that even happen?"

"People end up in that situation for so many different reasons," Eileen explained. "Sometimes they lose a job, or sometimes they have health issues and can't work. We try to help everyone who comes to the center, but we don't always have the resources."

"You need more donations?" I asked.

"Oh yes, definitely."

We said good-bye to Eileen and walked back to the Pleasant View Farm booth. Mom was handing out samples of the apple and pear compote she uses in a number of recipes at the restaurant. Cat was selling butternut squash, tomatoes, carrots, zucchini, and apples from our farm. Dad and Beckett had arrived. Dad brought a copy of the *Empire State Weddings* article, which he had framed. He set it up on an easel with a sign that read, CHECK OUT THE HUDSON VALLEY'S NEWEST EVENT SPACE.

I watched Mom, Dad, and Cat talk to the people who stopped at our booth. Many of them were friends and neighbors and people I'd known forever. Others were faces from the community that I recognized. I couldn't help wonder if some of these people were having trouble getting enough groceries each week. Were there other families I knew who were struggling like Abby and her dad? I was glad I could make recipe cards, but I wanted to do *more* to help.

Where was an idea-spark when I needed one?

꒕꒕꒕

In a small pen behind the booth, Beckett stood dressed in his silver sequined vest and black top hat. He and Dash ran through their tricks. It wasn't long before a crowd gathered to watch.

"Having Dash here was a genius idea," Cat whispered to me. "Our booth is getting more visitors than we've ever had at this festival!"

My brother got Dash to do his dance move, but in midstep, Dash dropped down to all fours and trotted over to the edge of the fence where a small boy was eating a hot dog. Dash started sniffing at the hot dog.

"Dash!" Beckett called. "That's not for you! *These* are for you!"

He shook the container of licorice treats. Dash turned around, and Beckett held up a hoop and shook the treats again.

Dash began running to the hoop. But instead of jumping through it, he ran around it and right back to where he'd come from: the boy with the hot dog.

CHOMP.

Before anyone could make a move, Dash had grabbed the rest of the hot dog and swallowed it down.

The crowd started laughing, but Dad hurried over

to the boy's parents. "We're really sorry about that," Dad said, holding out some money. "Please get another hot dog, on us." He turned to the boy. "You okay?"

"Are you kidding?" the boy replied, his eyes wide. "That was the most awesome thing that's ever happened to me!" The boy started clapping, and the rest of the crowd joined in.

Beckett grinned and took a bow.

CHAPTER 8
Like Oil and Water

W hat the heck?"

"Oh my gosh, what happened?"

I'd just rounded the corner of the school hallway and bumped into a crowd of kids gathered in the doorway of our classroom.

"What's going on?" I asked.

Thea turned around and pulled me into a spot next to her so I could see what they were looking at: our desks, rearranged into groups of four.

"Good morning, everyone," Ms. Lewis called, waving us in. "Please find your new spots."

Everyone started running through the room, searching for their desks. Amadi found hers and called, "Blaire! Over here! We're in the same group."

"Who else are we with?" I asked, walking over.

There was my desk, with the pencil holder I'd made

by wrapping an old soup can in red metallic duct tape. Right across from me was a desk with a sticker on it. In teeny-tiny type it said, IF YOU CAN READ THIS, PLEASE GET ME A DOUGHNUT.

I started laughing. "Whose desk is this?" I asked Amadi. She shrugged.

"It's mine," Eli said, coming up behind me.

"Oh. I like your sticker."

Eli flopped into his chair. He didn't look at me, or Amadi, or the other boy at our table, Lucas.

I slid into my own chair. "I didn't see you at the Harvest Festival," I said lightly. "Did you go?"

"Nope," Eli said.

"Oh. Well, what did you do on the weekend?"

Eli shrugged.

"Okay, class," Ms. Lewis called out to quiet us down. "Your desks will be in this setup for four weeks. I like to mix things up. And speaking of mixing, this morning's science lab is going to explore what we're learning about the density of liquids. You'll work with your desk group."

Ms. Lewis handed each table a liquid dropper, a tall plastic cup, and a stack of smaller plastic cups. Then she went around and filled our small cups with water, rubbing alcohol, honey, dish soap, vegetable oil, blue food coloring, and corn syrup.

"Add a drop of each liquid to the tall cup, starting with what you think is the most dense liquid. Talk amongst yourselves."

"I think that would be the honey," Lucas said to me, Amadi, and Eli.

"Maybe," Amadi said. "Or the corn syrup."

"Uh, no," Eli muttered. "It's the vegetable oil."

He grabbed the dropper and filled it with some of the oil, then added that to the cup. Next, he filled the dropper with corn syrup.

"Eli," I said. "We should be working together."

Eli just held up his palm, telling us to wait, and finished filling the dropper. He squeezed the syrup into the tall cup. It settled on top of the oil but didn't mix with it.

"That's so cool," Amadi said. "How did they stay separate?"

"The liquids are different densities," Eli said.

"Yeah," Lucas added. "That's why people say, 'those two are like oil and water' about people who don't really get along."

"Good call, Eli," I said. "You were right about vegetable oil."

"Uh-huh," Eli grunted. He got up and went to the pencil sharpener.

I looked at the jar where the liquids were settling on top of each other. Then I looked at Eli. He didn't seem to want to mix with anyone.

Well, I had four weeks to sit next to him. That gave me a lot of time to try to change that.

꿰꿰

At the end of the afternoon, we had a birthday circle for one of the girls in our class. Each of us had a turn telling Kristina what we admired about her. I said I liked how good she was at math and helped other people remember their facts when they needed. Then Kristina took out a big box filled with frosted sugar cookies. She started passing them around. When she got to me, she held the box out, but I didn't take a cookie.

"Don't you want one?" she asked.

"Is this . . . uh . . . dairy-free, by any chance?"

Kristina closed her eyes and bonked herself on the

forehead. "Oh my gosh, Blaire. I totally forgot that you can't have dairy! I'm so sorry!"

"It's okay," I said quietly. "I have my own cookies I can eat."

I didn't want Kristina to feel bad, especially on her birthday, but it felt awkward to get up and go to the storage cabinet for a different treat. I hoped no one was watching me.

When I got back to the circle, the other kids were eating their cookies, talking and laughing. No one said anything to me about my cookie, but I still felt awkward. I watched my friends lick frosting off their fingers like it was no big deal. For them, it wasn't. But it was for me.

That hurt my feelings as much as someone teasing me about the foods I couldn't eat.

CHAPTER 9
Operation Awesome Sauce

Cat and I were having our first "field date" since she'd gotten back from her honeymoon, and I was looking forward to our weekly time together. I waited for her by the greenhouse, eager to harvest some fall tomatoes and talk.

"Hey, Sprout! I'll be right out!" Cat called from inside, where she was washing off some tools in the sink.

While I waited, I checked over the row of onions that had been pulled out of the ground weeks ago and were now "curing" in the sun. Their white-brown skins made them look like a string of pearls. Nearby, there was the tomato field, dotted with red. In the distance, the ground was covered with the green flecks of zucchini.

I loved how the colors of growing food mixed together like confetti.

BOOM.

There it was. My idea-spark for Helping Hands!

"Cat!" I called. "I have to go do something! Be right back!"

"Hey," Cat shouted from the shed back. "What about our field date?"

"This. Can't. Wait."

I raced down the path, headed for the house. When I came around the side of the barn, I saw a delivery truck parked outside the restaurant's back door. Dad was helping the driver unload boxes as Mom made notes on a clipboard.

I ran into the family kitchen, where I knew the Helping Hands brochure was stuck on the fridge. Then I grabbed my tablet and sat down to write an email:

Dear Eileen,

I've been thinking a lot about what you said about food insecurity in our community. I have an idea!

Every year at the holidays, my family makes a homemade gift for our friends and neighbors with food that we've grown on the farm. Last year we made Veggie Confetti Sauce. It's a recipe my mom came up with for the restaurant, and it's full of good stuff like tomatoes, zucchini, carrots, onions, and peppers. It's great on pasta or even as a soup.

What if you had an event where volunteers made this sauce? I'm sure Pleasant View Farm could donate the vegetables, and we could give the sauce to the families at Helping Hands.

Sincerely,

Blaire Wilson

I went back out to the field to help Cat, eager to get Eileen's response.

As soon as Cat and I were done, I raced back inside to check my tablet. Eileen had written back:

Hi, Blaire,

I love that idea! But any canned items we distribute need to be prepared in a commercially certified kitchen to meet safety standards. Maybe we could use your mom's restaurant kitchen? And do you have volunteers in mind?

Thanks,

Eileen

The restaurant kitchen? That would be perfect! And did I have volunteers in mind? DUH. My class was full of kids still looking for a community service project.

Yes! I typed back.

Eileen's reply came almost immediately.

That sounds wonderful! Talk to your mom
and let me know what works for her schedule.
Then call me and we'll discuss details.

And suddenly, I knew it: I had found my official Community Service Challenge project.

I ran up to the inspiration board in my room. Abby's drawings were right in the middle. I touched them with my finger.

"Wait until Abby tries the Veggie Confetti Sauce," I told the little dog and the funny heart in the pictures. "I betcha her next drawing will be a bunch of happy dancing vegetables. You guys can all have a party right here on my wall!"

꧁꧂

That evening, I was doing my math homework in the family kitchen. For some reason, fractions were easier when I could listen to the hum of restaurant staff voices and the clink of dishes and glasses as everyone cleaned up in the dining room.

The door from the restaurant kitchen opened, and Mom and Dad appeared, looking serious.

"What's wrong?" I asked.

"Well," Mom said. "We just got a call from Eileen, at the Bluefield Helping Hands Center. She thanked us for hosting a 'Veggie Confetti Sauce'–making event."

Oh my gosh. I'd called Thea and told her all about it, but I hadn't talked to my parents yet.

"Sorry," I said. "You guys were busy with the delivery when I got my idea." I explained everything to Mom and Dad, expecting them to look excited. But they didn't.

"Blaire. That's not okay," Dad said in the voice he saved for times when he was really mad. "You absolutely *cannot* volunteer to host an event at the farm without checking with us first," he added.

I swallowed hard. "But it's going to be awesome, and the sauce will help so many families at the food pantry. Oh my gosh, we could change the name from Veggie Confetti to Awesome Sauce!"

"I'm sure it would be a wonderful project, Blaire," Mom said. "But with all the event reservations, our kitchen has gotten much busier."

"Oh," I said, sinking back down into my chair and wishing I could disappear into it. "I didn't think of that. Eileen said we needed a commercial kitchen, and I know we have one. I just—"

"—got caught up with your big idea-spark," Mom said, then she came over and crouched down so she was eye-to-eye with me. She put her hands on both my knees. "I know, sweetie. But big ideas are complicated."

Wait—was Mom saying no? So much for my Community Service Challenge project! Eileen was going to be so disappointed. And what about Abby and her dad and the other families at the food pantry?

"Isn't . . . can't . . ." I wasn't sure what to ask next.

A big lump was forming in my throat. I shot up from the table and headed for the back stairs, running fast until I reached the third floor.

When I got there, I flopped on my bed and stared at my inspiration board. Now what?

A few minutes later, there was a knock on the door and Mom and Dad came in.

"You left before we could finish the conversation," Dad said.

"Well, you said no."

Mom sat down on the bed beside me. "Not exactly. You stormed off before we finished talking. You missed something important. Plus, you were just plain rude."

"Sorry," I said. "What is the something important?"

"The kitchen is booked, but it's closed every Monday," Dad said. "That's your mom's day off."

"I'm willing to let you use the kitchen some Monday for your sauce event," Mom said.

I sat up. "You are?"

"That means your mom is giving up an evening of her own time," Dad said.

"You don't have to, Mom. I'll take care of everything."

Mom shook her head. "It's my kitchen. Nothing happens in there without me. Besides, you kids will need adults to supervise this project if you're going to donate the sauce. There are rules involved with food safety."

"This is a huge project, Blaire," Dad added. "You'll need to work with Cat to get the vegetables you need."

"No problem," I said.

"And you'll need jars," Mom added. "Do you have money to buy them?"

"Um . . . I haven't gotten that far yet," I admitted.

Mom and Dad looked at each other. "All right, Blaire-with-the-big-ideas," Dad said with a sigh. "I'll help you figure that one out."

"Thank you!" I jumped up and pulled Mom and Dad into a group hug. "This is for a really great cause—and it will be even more fun doing it together! Operation Awesome Sauce is on!"

CHAPTER 10

Big Just Got Bigger

O n Monday morning, I stood inside the front doors
of school. Thea and I took different buses, so we
always waited for each other next to the community service display case. I looked at the photo of her cousin
George's doghouse—the one he'd made with all the cans
of dog food he'd collected for the animal shelter. I
bounced on my toes, imagining Operation Awesome
Sauce included in the case.

WHAM! Someone crashed into me.

"Ow!" I cried.

It was Eli. Two boys from another class laughed
and high-fived each other. I could tell they'd just
pushed him.

"Next time, don't take our seat on the bus," one said
as they walked away.

Eli steadied himself. He'd dropped his backpack, and stuff had spilled out all over the floor.

I bent down to help him. I picked up a copy of *The Lion, the Witch and the Wardrobe*, one of my favorite books. "Are you okay?" I asked.

He looked at me and blinked hard. Then he shrugged and took his book.

"I'm sorry about those guys," I said. "They're total bus bullies."

"Whatever," Eli said, turning to go.

Suddenly, I was annoyed that Eli never finished a conversation. "Wait," I said. "Why won't you let someone be your friend?"

Eli stopped and turned around to face me. "Do you really think I'm not *letting* anyone be my friend?"

"It kind of seems that way," I said gently. "People want to get to know you. At least, I do. I'm sure other kids do, too."

Eli nodded. "Okay," he said, then headed up the stairs.

Okay . . . Did that mean he was going to try and be more friendly?

I hoped so. Somewhere in there was a funny kid who made videos, like I did, read the same kinds of books as

I did, and had who-knows-what-else in common with me. Maybe someday soon, I'd find out.

⁂

"Okay, my friends!" Ms. Lewis began. "Blaire has something she'd like to share with us. Blaire, take it from here."

"So," I began. "You all know the Bluefield Helping Hands Center, right? They have a lot of families who come to their food pantry for help with groceries, but the center doesn't always have enough supplies. I have an idea about how we could help change that."

Just saying the word *change* made me even more excited to share my plan. "I love to cook, so I thought of a way to cook for the people who visit the food pantry, by making a yummy pasta sauce. I call it Awesome Sauce. But I need help. I need some volunteers to come to Pleasant View Farm on Sunday to harvest the vegetables and herbs we'd need for the sauce and make labels for the jars. Then on Monday, when the restaurant kitchen is closed, we can use it to clean and prep the veggies, cook the sauce, and put it in jars."

I paused and looked around. Would anyone be as excited as I was? "I'm going to send around a sign-up sheet," I said, picking up a clipboard. "There are two columns—one for each of the days."

"Can people sign up for both days?" Ms. Lewis asked.

"Sure," I replied.

As the clipboard made its way around the room, Ms. Lewis asked questions about Helping Hands. Soon the whole class was talking about the center and how long it had been part of the community. Everyone knew it was a place people could get clothes and household items, but a lot of kids didn't know about the food pantry.

"How much sauce are you planning to make, Blaire?" Ms. Lewis asked.

"Well," I said, "my dad and I talked to the manager at the hardware store, and he's going to donate one hundred jars. So my goal is to fill them all."

"That's, uh, a lot of jars," Sabrina said.

Ms. Lewis nodded. "That's very ambitious, Blaire."

"I know. But there are at least that many people who visit the pantry every week. And if we can do it . . . that'll be . . ."

"Epic!" Amadi chimed in with her favorite word, and a bunch of us laughed.

When the clipboard got back to me, everyone in the room had signed up for at least one of the days. Even Eli.

"Well," Ms. Lewis said, looking over my shoulder at the clipboard. "It's now official: We have a class-wide Community Service Challenge project! You know, nobody's done that in a while. This is unique. *And* challenging. I can't wait to see how you pull this off."

That made two of us.

⟡

After school, when I headed home to set up our daily afternoon coffee, tea, and cookies service for the B-and-B guests, I found Marco in the sitting room, surrounded by paint swatches.

"Hello, Blaire!" he called. "This room has the perfect light for looking at color samples."

"I guess I never noticed that," I said. "How are things at the Masons' house?"

"Fabulous. We're going to start working on the kids'

bedrooms next," Marco said. "I would love, love, love for you to come and brainstorm with me."

Redesigning a kid's bedroom? DUH, yes, please! I had only a couple dozen things on my inspiration board for that, and so many idea-sparks stored in my brain, I couldn't count them.

"Yeah!" I said. "Anytime."

"Sunday?" Marco asked.

"Of course," I replied. "Oh—wait." My heart sank. "That's the day my class is coming over to pick vegetables. We're making pasta sauce for the food pantry," I explained. There was no way I could go with Marco.

"Well, I'm going over in the morning if you can join me," Marco said. Then his cell phone rang. He answered it and began speaking to someone in Spanish.

In the morning? The kids weren't coming until after lunch. So I *could* go to the Masons' house and still be back in time for all the prep stuff. Maybe I didn't have to choose.

I caught Marco's eye and nodded. He gave me a thumbs-up. This was going to be *super-bonita*!

CHAPTER 11

Prep Day

"Here's a copy of the schedule," I said to Cat, handing her a sheet of paper. We were sitting on the porch swing, going over the plan for the afternoon. My classmates were coming over at one o'clock and I wanted to make sure everything was organized before Marco and I left for the set.

"Wow, Blaire," Cat said, skimming the schedule. "You've got it all planned out."

I nodded. "Since I'll be gone this morning, I wanted to make sure everything is ready to go."

Cat looked up from her paper. "You're leaving?"

I nodded. "I'm going with Marco to the Masons' house. I'll only be gone for a few hours."

"When are you going to pick the produce your mom needs for tonight's dinner service?" Cat asked. "Remember you promised to do that."

Oh no. I *had* made that promise, and those ingredients had to be in the kitchen by noon so Mom could start prepping. "I'm sorry. I spaced out on that. It's just that Marco invited me to work on the kids' bedrooms. Do you, um, have time to get what Mom needs?"

Cat shook her head. "I'm helping the Martins with their booth at the Elleville farmers' market this morning, remember?"

I hadn't remembered that either. I was wondering if I could possibly beg Beckett to do the field work for me when Marco came out the front door. *"Buenos días,* ladies! Blaire, are you ready? Suzanne should be here any minute to pick us up."

Cat just stared at me, one eyebrow raised, while Marco checked his phone. When a car pulled into the driveway, I thought it was Suzanne. But the back door opened and Abby exploded out.

"Blaire!" she called, running up to the porch to give me a hug.

"Hey!" I said, squeezing her back, trying to hide my surprise. I'd invited Abby to join us this afternoon, but she was early.

"I got called in to work," Abby's dad explained as he

walked toward us from the car. "I asked your mom if I could drop Abby off now to play with Beckett."

"Oh!" I said. "That's . . . great. Abby, Beckett's inside somewhere. Go find him."

Abby dashed into the house. I really, really wanted to follow her. I'd planned to show her all the secrets of the house and farm, starting with the hidden play kitchen Dad and I had built under the stairs, but now I wouldn't be around for that.

Abby's dad left just as Suzanne arrived.

"Okay!" Marco said. "Off we go!"

That was my cue to follow him. I tried to take a step off the porch, but there was a heavy feeling in my stomach and my feet didn't move.

"Um, Marco? I . . . er . . . can't go with you today."

"Why not?" he asked, looking puzzled.

"I've organized a project with my class for this afternoon and I promised Cat I'd help with the restaurant harvest this morning." *And now Abby's here*, I thought. "I'm sorry. I can't help at the house today."

Marco frowned. "That is a shame for me and for the show. But it's clear that your *corazón* is in the right place. We have to listen to our hearts, yes?"

"Definitely," I said. "Thanks for understanding."

He nodded and raced down the steps into Suzanne's car.

Cat tugged on my ponytail as she walked into the house. "Good choice, Sprout. See you this afternoon."

⁂

"That's a *chicken*?" my classmate Joey said. He wrinkled his nose at Dandelion when I held her up for everyone to see. "It looks like someone put it through the wash and it came out all fluffy."

"It's a Silkie chicken," I explained, then turned to Abby standing next to me. "Abby, would you like to go in and check the nesting boxes for me? See if anyone left an egg for us?"

Abby, Beckett, and I had been all over the farm that morning. They had helped me gather produce for the restaurant, and Abby helped Mom and me make lunch. Abby played with Dash and Penelope, and Grandpa gave us all a tractor ride. But the thing Abby loved the most was the chickens. I'd shown her how to gather eggs, and she was delighted to find that they were warm when she picked them from the nest.

My classmates were amazed with the chickens, too. As everyone arrived, they gravitated to the coop to watch the birds.

Now Abby gave me a quick nod as I opened the gate. She came out of the nesting shed a minute later holding a small blue-gray egg.

"Why isn't it white?" Eli asked.

"Chickens lay eggs of all different colors," I said. "It depends on their breed."

"This one probably came from one of our Ameraucana hens," Grandpa added. "Some people call them Easter Egg Chickens!"

"Can I see it?" Joey asked, reaching for the egg. He grabbed it before Abby could even answer, but it flipped out of his fingers. Eli moved in a flash to catch it right before it hit the ground.

"Save!" he said, holding up the egg.

"Give it to me," Joey said.

"I don't think Abby was done with it yet," Eli told him, putting the egg carefully back in Abby's palm. She gave him a huge smile.

Thea came up beside me. "Who is that kid?" she whispered. "It's like he's a totally different person here than at school."

"I was just thinking the same thing," I replied.

Eli was his usual shy self when he first arrived at the farm, but as soon as he met Beckett and Abby, he was much more talkative. Beckett thought Eli was totally cool because his T-shirt had a goat in a pool wearing water wings and the words GOATS DON'T FLOAT.

"Okay, farm crew!" Cat called. "Are you ready to pick some vegetables?"

Everyone cheered, except for Eli, who took out his tablet and started shooting video.

"That's weird," Thea whispered.

"Well, he did say he likes to make videos," I said as we all headed to the fields.

It took us a while to gather all the vegetables and herbs we needed, but everyone seemed to have a great time. It helped that Grandpa told funny stories about growing up on the farm, and that Cat came up with a who-can-find-the-strangest-looking-carrot contest. Abby won when she pulled one out of the ground and announced that it looked like a troll with three legs.

As we all headed back to the house, Abby slipped her hand in mind. "I can't wait to try the sauce you make with these veggies," she said. "It's going to be awesome to eat something with vegetables I helped pick."

Awesome indeed.

CHAPTER 12

Sauce Day

"Happy birrrrrth-daaaaay, dear Eeeee-liiii!" we all sang on Monday afternoon. "Happy birthday to youuuuu!"

I leaned over to Thea, who was sitting next to me in our circle on the carpet. "I can't believe Eli's birthday was yesterday. Why didn't he say something at the farm?"

"Because he's a MAN OF MYSTERY," Thea whispered back.

Eli didn't want our class to do the "What I Admire About Eli" part of the birthday circle, so as soon as the singing stopped, he started handing out the treat he'd brought.

"My mom made chocolate chip brownies," he said, passing the first one to Lucas. He began making his way around the circle. I got up to get a cookie from home.

But suddenly, Eli was next to me. "These, uh, are actually dairy-free brownies."

"They are?" I couldn't hide my surprise. "That's really nice. Thank you." I took a brownie.

"Thank my mom," Eli said, shrugging and moving on to offer a brownie to Thea. "I told her there was a girl in my class who couldn't eat dairy, so she found a special recipe."

I took a bite. It was delicious to be eating the same thing everyone else was eating.

As we walked out of school that day, I caught up with Eli.

"It was really nice that you told your mom about the dairy-free thing," I said. "Not everyone does that."

"Well . . . it was nice that you invited everyone to your farm," he replied.

"So, uh, why didn't you tell anyone it was your birthday yesterday?"

"It felt weird to make a big deal out of it," he said, with one of his famous shrugs. "Besides, I was already having a good day. It was fun to hang out with everyone. Especially Abby and your brother."

"Beckett said you were really nice."

Eli smiled. "I like little kids. I have a bunch of younger cousins in California. I miss hanging out with them."

Wow. That was the most Eli had told me about his family. I started to ask a question when Eli said, "See you tonight."

And with that, he disappeared into the crowds heading for the buses.

I smiled. Were Eli and I becoming friends?

✺

I rushed home to help Mom and Dad prep the tomatoes. By the time all the Sauce Day volunteers had arrived, Mom and I had the tomatoes ready to simmer, and Cat and Grandpa had sterilized all the jars.

My classmates gathered in the bistro dining room. "Who's ready to make some Awesome Sauce?" I asked, and everyone cheered—including the grown-ups. Having everyone together, ready to make something big happen, gave me a flutter of excitement.

"All right!" I continued. "Thanks for remembering to wear bandannas."

"Hair is not one of the ingredients in Awesome Sauce," Eli said quietly, making everyone laugh.

"There's a team list at each of the prep stations in the kitchen," I continued. "Find your spot, and make sure you wash your hands before we start. Let's go!"

Mom led the group into the kitchen, and everyone took a moment to look around. "This," a boy named Mark said, "is the shiniest kitchen I've ever seen."

"This used to be the house's living room, if you can believe that!" I said.

Everyone washed up and found their stations. Dad, Cat, and Grandpa were each at one of the chopping stations, and Mom was at the stove. I darted around the room, making sure everyone had what they needed. At the onion table, I handed out swim goggles to Thea and the other kids, so their eyes wouldn't tear up from chopping.

Thea put on her goggles, held up an onion, and said, "I come from Planet Sauce-tron. What are these strange food items that make earthlings cry?" Then Thea leaned in and whispered to me, "Isn't it time to start your Operation Awesome Sauce playlist?"

"What makes you think I have a special playlist?" I asked.

Thea raised an eyebrow at me. "Uh, because you're Blaire. You always have a special playlist."

I smiled at her, then found my tablet and speaker and started the music.

Before I knew it, everyone was singing along to the first song, and the sounds of *chop chop chop* added a beat. At the carrots table, I saw Eli and David joking about something again.

"Hey, Blaire!" David said, calling me over. "Eli just came up with new lyrics for that song. Do it again, Eli."

Eli looked embarrassed for a moment, then took a deep breath and started singing to the tune of the song's chorus.

"Carrots . . . carrots . . . they give us all the feels. We got kick, and we got crunch . . . and we also have great peels . . ."

Everyone burst out laughing.

"Eli! That's perfect!" Thea said.

"Hey!" I called out. "Let's have a vegetable theme song contest! My grandpa can be the judge."

"Only if the winning team gets a pass on cleanup!" Joey answered.

"Deal," I said.

A few minutes later, Joey's team sang their song. *"Zucchini . . . Zucchini! You can eat it in a bikini! Don't confuse it with a cucumber, you should really call it squash . . . It's the color of an alligator but it really tastes top-notch!"*

I started cracking up, and glanced back over to the carrots team. *Wait a sec*—Eli wasn't peeling carrots anymore. He was holding up his tablet and taking video of the rest of his team doing all the work. I went over to his table.

"Um, Eli," I said, tapping him on the arm. "What are you doing?"

Eli shrugged. "I want to take some video of Sauce Day. Is that okay?"

"Uh . . . sure. I guess. Just don't get in anyone's way."

"An interview's more interesting if it's in the middle of the action," Eli replied.

"Well, just for a few minutes, then. We really need everyone to keep chopping."

But Eli didn't seem to hear me. He was circling the

table, taking video of his group working on the carrots. Then he started interviewing Lucas.

I went to the back of the kitchen, where Mom was at the stove, overseeing six large pots of simmering tomato sauce. "How's it going?" I asked Mom.

"Great!" she said, waving a big wooden spoon at me. "We'll be ready for veggies in about five minutes."

"Got it," I said, turning around. *OOF.*

I bumped into Eli.

"Sorry," he said from behind his tablet. "I was just getting footage of the sauce."

"Be careful," Mom said. "This is very hot."

Eli backed away. "Right."

"Are the carrots ready?" I asked Eli.

"Carrots? Not sure. Let's go check." Eli put his tablet down.

There were still a dozen carrots to peel and chop. I sighed, picked up a peeler and a carrot, and got to work.

"Wow," Eli said. "That's the fastest peeling I've ever seen."

"My mom taught me," I said. Then I smiled. "We used to have races to see who could finish first."

"So did your mom inspire you to do this project?" Eli asked.

I kept peeling as I answered. "She inspired me to like cooking. But it was Abby who inspired me to do this project."

"Tell me about it," Eli said.

So I told him about meeting Abby and how I realized she'd like veggies if she had a chance to try some and that my goal for this sauce was to help other families at Helping Hands try new foods, too.

I looked up, expecting to see Eli chopping, but he was holding his tablet. He hadn't been helping at all. He'd been filming me! "Eli!" I said, totally exasperated.

"Blaire, it's time for veggies," Mom called to me.

I looked around the room to see that all the other teams were done with their vegetable prep. But there were still carrots to chop.

I called Thea and Rosie over. "Can you guys help finish here? They ended up shorthanded." I glared at Eli, who was facing the other way, interviewing Cat.

"We're on it," Thea said.

I turned to see that Eli was headed for the stove. As

Mom moved a pot of tomatoes to another burner, Eli started walking toward her.

He was totally going to get in Mom's way! I raced toward him.

But I stumbled, knocking into Mom's shoulder. She lost her hold on the sauce, and the pot tipped over. All three of us jumped back as hot red liquid started spilling out.

"Whoa!" someone shouted.

Thinking fast, Mom grabbed the pot and was able to set it upright again. But most of the sauce was now on the floor. It looked like a volcano had erupted and lava was oozing through our restaurant kitchen.

No, no, no, no, no. This couldn't be happening! We'd never get one hundred jars of sauce now!

Mom, Dad, and Cat raced to start cleaning up. Grandpa gathered the other kids out of the way.

Eli had backed up against the wall, wiping sauce off his tablet. Was that all he cared about? I stomped over to him.

"Look what you did!" I snapped. "Now we're not going to have enough sauce!"

"What *I* did?" he asked. "You're the one who made it spill!"

"But you've been in everyone's way today!" I shot back at him. "Doing that video stuff instead of helping!"

"Yeah," Kristina added. "It was kind of annoying having you in our faces with your tablet while we were trying to work."

"Maybe you don't care about this project, but we do," Sabrina chimed in.

Eli looked at Sabrina, then at me, then at the tablet in his hand. Without saying a word, he took off, past the rest of the class, out of the kitchen. I heard the front door slam. Everyone was silent for a long moment.

"I'll go check on him," Dad said, and left the room.

I turned to Mom, feeling like I was going to cry. She put her arm around me.

"Okay, chefs," Mom said. "Unexpected disasters happen all the time in professional kitchens. Right now we need to finish the sauce so we can fill the jars and get them sealed."

Mom leaned close to my ear. "Everyone's going to follow your lead here, Blaire."

I knew what she was saying. Even though I felt like giving up, I had to keep going. We couldn't let one mistake ruin the whole project.

I picked up a bowl of carrots and did my best to smile. "Come on. Let's finish Operation Awesome Sauce."

CHAPTER 13

A Jarring Experience

Cat and I arrived at Helping Hands with seventy-six jars of Awesome Sauce. I'd wanted to make another batch so we could get to our goal of one hundred, but Mom and the kitchen were too busy the rest of the week, and there weren't enough vegetables anyway.

Eli had been absent from school on Tuesday and Wednesday, after our fight on Sauce Day. When he came back, he was even quieter than normal, and we managed to go all day Thursday and Friday without talking. I kept thinking he was going to apologize, and we could go back to being sort-of friends again. But he didn't.

Eileen came outside with a cart to meet Cat and me.

"We're so excited that you're here. I'll help you unload."

The three of us transferred boxes of sauce, along with the donation of fresh produce, into the food pantry.

"I set up a table for you and your sauce," she said.

"Thanks," Cat said. "Sprout, you handle the jars, and I'll get the fruits and veggies sorted."

I'd brought along a tablecloth and a mason jar of wildflowers from the farm. I also had recipe cards with ideas for how to use our Awesome Sauce. As I set up the table, I was eager to see Abby. I wanted to make sure she got a jar of sauce.

A little while later, Eileen poked her head in the door. "We're about to open up. You guys ready?"

"A hundred percent," I said, spreading my arms out to indicate the arrangement of jars on the table.

A mom with a baby and a toddler came in first. She signed in on a clipboard hanging on the wall, then immediately came over to our table.

"What's all this?" she asked.

I explained all about the sauce, and how my class made it from fresh ingredients grown on our farm.

The mom picked up a jar and looked at the label. "Wow," she murmured as she read. "My Italian grandmother used to make something like this. Comfort food!"

"It totally is," I said. "Here, take a recipe card with it!"

"This is perfect," the woman said. "My dad turns seventy next week. I'd love to make him a special meal, and maybe this'll remind him of his mom's cooking. Thank you so much."

"You're welcome."

As the woman and her kids walked away, Cat turned to me. "You really made her day."

"I hope so," I said.

Several more families and an elderly couple came in and took jars of sauce before they moved on to fill up the rest of their grocery bags. Lots of people had stories about the gardens and fresh vegetables they had, or their grandparents had, growing up.

"There's nothing like a tomato fresh from the garden," an older man said. He reminded me of Grandpa.

"Well, this sauce will make you feel like you're eating fresh tomatoes," I said.

"You're so sweet," his wife said. "Can I give you a hug?"

"Absolutely!" I said, walking around the table for a big squeeze.

It seemed like everyone who visited the pantry came over to our table. Cat and I talked to people nonstop. But where was Abby? She and her dad usually got in line early. I hoped something hadn't happened to hold them up. I also hoped we didn't run out of sauce before they got here. I grabbed a jar and stashed it under the table for them, just in case.

"Hey, Cat," I said, wanting to tell her about the jar I was saving for Abby. But she was talking to a volunteer. I was about to tap Cat on the shoulder when I heard someone call my name.

"Blaire Wilson, is that you?" I turned to see a woman grinning at me. "You probably don't remember me, but my daughter Peggy used to work at your mom's restaurant. You were just a little thing back then, running around the farm, greeting guests. You've grown so much! What's in all these jars?"

"I think I do remember you!" I said, and went on to tell her about how we'd cooked up the sauce in the same kitchen her daughter knew so well.

The line kept flowing fast into the room, with

people coming up to our table to get jars and thank us. We went through one box of jars, and then another, and still . . . there was no sign of Abby. I was getting pretty worried. By the time we'd given away most of the last box, I couldn't take the wondering any longer. Had Abby even shown up at all?

"Be right back," I told Cat, walking toward the doorway. I saw people lined up all the way down the hall. My heart sank. If we hadn't spilled that pot of sauce, we might have had enough for everyone. Now I knew for sure we were going to run out.

"Blaire!" I heard Abby's voice call.

"There you are!" I said as I found her and her dad in the line.

"Our car broke down so we had to get a ride," she said.

"That's okay," I told her, taking her hand. "Come on, I have a jar of sauce set aside just for you."

We left Abby's dad holding their place in line, and I brought her into the food pantry room. Cat was gathering up the empty boxes. I reached under the table, feeling for her jar . . . but it wasn't there.

"Hold on a sec," I told Abby, and bent down to look all the way under the table.

The jar was gone.

I stood back up and turned to Cat. "What happened to the jar of sauce that was down here?"

"I just gave it away," Cat said. "I thought we'd run out, and then I spotted that one."

I felt an instant lump in my throat, but swallowed it down. Cat saw the look on my face and asked, "Was I not supposed to do that?"

"I was saving it for Abby."

"Oh my gosh, Blaire! Abby! I'm sorry!"

"No, it's my fault," I said, shaking my head. "I meant to tell you, but we were busy and I didn't get a chance."

"You mean there's no more Awesome Sauce?" Abby asked.

I sank down onto the chair so I was eye level with Abby. "So many people came to the food pantry today, and we didn't have as many jars as we planned."

Abby bit her lip. "But you promised me. You said the Awesome Sauce would be my new favorite food."

"I know. I'll make some more."

"But I wanted the sauce made from the vegetables

I helped pick." Abby looked down at the floor. Her shoulders sagged. It was like she was a balloon and someone had just let all the air out of her. "I guess I'll go back to my dad."

She walked slowly out of the room, pausing at the door to look back at me with a face full of disappointment.

I stood there frozen, not sure what to do next, when Eileen came over, and Cat explained what happened.

"Oh, Blaire. That's unfortunate. But Abby will be okay. It's just not so fun for these families, week after week. And our line seems to get longer every Saturday."

"I can't believe we didn't have enough sauce for everyone," I said, fighting back tears. "I'm really sorry."

"Don't apologize! What you did was absolutely wonderful. Every jar helped someone."

I nodded, but inside, I felt like I was deflating, just like Abby. I thought of the pot of sauce that had gone to waste. Then I thought of Eli. If he hadn't been shooting video, he wouldn't have been in Mom's way and that pot wouldn't have spilled. We would have another twenty-four jars of sauce, and Abby would have gotten one.

The first thing I was going to do in school on Monday was ask Ms. Lewis to move my desk as far away from Eli's as she could.

CHAPTER 14

Officially Friends?

As soon as I walked into class on Monday morning, everyone wanted to know how things had gone at Helping Hands. So Ms. Lewis had everyone sit down on the rug for Monday Madness. "Tell us about Saturday, Blaire," she said.

I looked at Eli and thought of the sauce that had been ruined last week. But then I thought about what Mom had said in the kitchen. Everyone was watching for *my* reaction.

"It was great," I said. I told the class how much everyone appreciated the sauce and how many people were happy to have something that was made from fresh, local produce. "We could have given away another hundred jars," I said.

After Monday Madness, Eli and I were face-to-face at our desks.

"I'm glad it went well," he said.

"It didn't," I answered coldly. "We didn't have enough for everyone. Abby didn't even get a jar. Because of you."

He frowned, confused. "How is that because of me?"

"You messed up the Sauce Day with all your video stuff."

Eli's face fell. "You're the one who knocked into your mom!"

I sighed, shaking my head. "Everyone else was helping, and you weren't. Abby was so disappointed."

I turned away from Eli without saying another word.

⚘

At home that afternoon, I moved Penelope and Dash's paddock to an enclosure by the orchard. That would give them a chance to graze on different grasses, which was good for their tummies. It was also a way to put Dash to work doing something super-useful: eating poison ivy and other plants in places we didn't want. Goats aren't allergic to poison ivy the way people are.

"That's the cutest weed-whacker ever," a voice said from behind an apple tree.

"Hi, Marco," I called. "Doing your thinking here today?"

"Yes, indeed," he replied from where he was sitting against a tree. "And I was just thinking about your big project. How did everyone like the sauce?"

"They liked it . . . or at least the ones who got some did. We didn't have enough for everyone." I walked over to Marco and sat down across from him. "I barely made a difference at all."

"How many jars of sauce did you give out?" Marco asked.

"Seventy-six."

Marco shook his head and smiled. "Seventy-six jars sounds like a big difference. Besides, it's the smallest amounts that become the biggest amounts."

"What do you mean?"

"When I was growing up in Mexico, my father owned a construction company. He scheduled one hour every week for himself. Do you know what he did during that time?"

I shook my head.

"He did house repairs for people who could not afford to pay him. As soon as I got old enough, he let me work with him. That was how I learned to make old things new again. But we only had one hour each week, and often it wasn't enough time to fix a problem."

I nodded. I knew how that felt.

"So every week, we went back. We kept working on the same problem until it was fixed. Sometimes it would take two weeks, and sometimes it would take two months. However long, my father did not give up."

Marco was quiet for a while. I thought about the seventy-six families we had helped with our sauce.

"There is no helping that's too small, Blaire," Marco said, standing up. "Maybe you have to go back and do some more, but that doesn't mean the first bit didn't count."

"I hadn't thought of it that way," I said quietly. "Thanks, Marco."

"You're welcome. You see—a different perspective can make all the difference." With that, Marco stood up and brushed off the seat of his jeans. Suddenly, I jumped up, too.

"Marco, wait!" I cried. "From my perspective, I see poison ivy. You've been sitting in it!"

Dash wandered over and started eating the clump Marco had been sitting on. "So *now* you show up?" Marco said to the goat.

"*Maaaah*," Dash said with his mouth full.

Marco looked at me and we both started laughing.

⚬

At school the next morning, Ms. Lewis announced that Eli had something he wanted to share with the class. He glanced nervously at me before going over to the class computer. I hadn't said a word to him since the day before.

After a moment, a picture came up on the Smart Board at the front of the room. White letters against a dark red background. THIS IS OPERATION AWESOME SAUCE.

OMG. Was Eli actually going to show us the videos he made during Prep Day and Sauce Day? That was pretty much the last thing I wanted to see.

The video started with some shots of the Bluefield Helping Hands Center from the outside. Then there were images of the food pantry shelves and the mostly empty refrigerator where fresh produce is stored. When had Eli gotten those shots?

Next were some things he shot from our Prep Day. There were the chickens, and Penny and Dash, and then everyone pulling carrots and picking zucchini. Dad was explaining how we got donations of mason jars from the local hardware store. The way the video was edited, it was clear that lots of people had come together to make this project happen.

Then the screen faded to black. When it lit up again, there was a girl on the screen.

Just like when I watched the *Room Revolutions* video, it took me a second to realize, that girl was me.

I was peeling carrots, talking about how I'd come up with the idea for Operation Awesome Sauce. Eli had added music, which made what I was saying seem even more dramatic. Then the video cut away to a shot of me and Abby walking through the orchard on Prep Day. You could only see the backs of our heads, but I could tell it was us. Abby reached out and took my hand.

The rest of the video showed the kids in our class picking and chopping the vegetables, and Mom stirring the pots of simmering tomatoes in the restaurant kitchen.

The video ended with another shot of the Helping Hands Center. Eli zoomed in on a family walking out of the building, holding bags of groceries. The final screen said, THE BLUEFIELD HELPING HANDS CENTER NEEDS MORE HELPING HANDS! LET'S GET MORE CANNED FOOD TO OUR NEIGHBORS WHO NEED IT!

Below that was the website and phone number of the center.

When it ended, we all sat there for a few seconds. The room was totally silent.

Wow, I thought. *Eli is really good at this video stuff.*

I started clapping and everyone joined in.

"Awesome video, bro!" someone said.

"That was epic," Amadi added.

Eli shrugged, but he also smiled.

✳

For the first time since he came to our school, Eli wasn't sitting alone in the cafeteria. All the boys in our class squeezed into his regular table at lunch, asking him questions about how he had made the video. His face lit up as he was talking, and the other boys were laughing.

When we came outside for recess, the boys invited him to play basketball with them, but he shook his head and went to sit in his usual spot, by a tree near the edge of the playground.

"Come on, Blaire," Thea said, tugging on my jacket sleeve. "Race you up the spiderweb."

"I'll be there in a minute," I told her.

Thea went off to join our other friends, and I headed over to the tree. When Eli looked up and saw me, he actually rolled his eyes.

"What do *you* want?"

I took a deep breath. "I want to apologize."

Eli looked surprised.

"You were right," I said softly. "Spilling the sauce was at least partly my fault. I'm sorry I got so mad."

Eli stared at me for a few seconds. "Thanks," he finally said. "I'm sorry my videoing got in the way."

I pointed to the ground next to him, asking if I could sit. He shrugged again. I was learning that a shrug was Eli language for *Yeah, let's talk more.*

So I sat down and said, "Your video was really great."

"Thanks," Eli murmured.

"I had no idea you went to Helping Hands."

"Before I went, I didn't really get how many people needed help."

"Yeah, me neither."

We were quiet for a moment. I picked some dirt out of the sole of my sneaker, and Eli started tugging at a weed in the grass.

"So what are you going to do with that video now?" I asked. "Are you going to show it to Eileen?"

"I don't know," Eli said. "I guess so. But I didn't make it for anyone besides our class. Really I just made it for myself. And for my—"

He stopped and bit his lip.

"And for my dad," he continued. Then he took a deep breath. It sounded shaky, as if he were about to cry. "He died last year."

"Oh . . ." I said, not sure what to say next. "Gosh, Eli. That's awful."

"That's why we moved here. To be near my mom's family."

"You said you made the video partly for him," I said. "What did you mean?"

"Well," Eli began, tugging at the weed again. "He's the one who taught me how to do all that. We, um, made videos together all the time. We'd post them on a private account and send them around to our online friends. We had a whole group of people on a message board who were like us, who loved making videos."

"That's really neat," I said. "Do other kids know about your dad?"

"No. It's not like I'm going to get a T-shirt that says, MY DAD DIED, FEEL SORRY FOR ME. Ms. Lewis and the principal know, though."

"You must miss him a lot."

Eli nodded. "All the time. You know what's weird? This is the first place I've made a video since he got sick. And the first one I made without him."

"Really?"

"Yeah. I just started taking video of Bluefield whenever I was driving around with my mom, pretending I was showing our new town to my dad. That was another thing me and my dad used to do before he got sick. We moved around a lot for his job, and we'd get to know the town by driving all over and taking video of it."

Eli paused, staring at the sky. I thought of him and his dad, exploring those other towns they lived in.

"Then," Eli continued, "at your farm, I pretended I was showing him the kids in my new class and what we were doing for Operation Awesome Sauce."

"I can't imagine moving around that much," I said, finally telling him what I'd been thinking since he first arrived. "I've only ever lived here. Wasn't it hard to leave your friends every time?"

He shrugged. "I never really had any friends. Wherever we went, I knew we'd only be there for maybe a year, so it seemed pointless to try. My dad was my best friend, anyway."

Eli tugged really hard on the weed this time, and it finally popped out of the ground. We both looked at it in his open palm.

"If you're going to stay in Bluefield," I said, "you can make friends now."

"I'm not very good at it," he said, then looked right in my eyes. "I'm not good at being part of things."

"You were part of Operation Awesome Sauce . . ."

"I still feel different from everyone else," Eli said. "Like no one really gets what it's like . . . to be me, I guess."

"I feel different from everyone else, too," I said.

"Because of the dairy thing?"

I nodded. "It feels really weird to eat something different when everyone else gets to eat yummy stuff with milk and cheese in it. My mom says it'll get easier."

Eli smiled a little. "My mom says that, too. About missing my dad."

"Oh my gosh," I said, suddenly horrified, because my being dairy-free felt like nothing compared to losing a parent. "I didn't mean . . . I mean, I know me being dairy-free is not as serious as—"

Eli shrugged. "It's not, like, a contest," he said. He flipped the weed over in his hand. "What's the hardest part about being dairy-free?"

"Feeling left out of things," I replied. "And other kids don't always get that I feel that way. They don't understand what it's like, so they'll accidentally say or do something that makes me feel even worse. It was really cool when you brought in those dairy-free brownies, because for once, I wasn't different."

Eli nodded. "It's a huge bummer, feeling different."

"Ms. Lewis wants me to talk about all that with the whole class. Maybe I should. Or maybe I could just get a shirt that says, PLEASE REMEMBER THAT I CAN'T EAT DAIRY AND THAT IT MAKES ME FEEL WEIRD SOMETIMES."

Now Eli laughed. At something I said!

Yes, it had happened.

Eli and I were officially friends.

CHAPTER 15

Best Room Makeover Ever

few days later, I was covering the front desk for
Grandpa when the phone rang.

"Pleasant View Farm," I said. "May I help you?"

"Hi, Blaire."

I recognized the voice. "Eileen! Hi!"

"Blaire, something really exciting is happening,"
Eileen said.

I pictured a blimp hovering over the Helping Hands
Center, dropping crates of food attached to little
parachutes.

"Did you see Eli's video?" she asked.

"Yes! Did he send it to you? It's great, right?"

"I cried the first five times I watched it," she said

with a little laugh. "He told the story of our food pantry and our challenges so well. I asked him if I could post it on the Helping Hands social media pages, and he said yes, so we put it up last night. Guess how many emails I had in my inbox this morning?"

"Ummm . . . I'm guessing, a lot?"

"Over three hundred! The video's been viewed over a thousand times and the number of shares goes up every hour. It's crazy!"

"That's great that people are sharing it."

"They're also really inspired by it. People are stepping up. I've received so many inquiries from people and groups wanting to organize donations. Folks asking how to volunteer. And a lot of them are really interested in getting involved in more canning events like Operation Awesome Sauce."

"More helping!" I cried. "That's amazing news." But then my excitement faded. "But I don't think we can use the Pleasant View Farm kitchen anytime soon."

"So we'll find somewhere else," Eileen said, her voice sounding cheerful and confident. "Would you still help out even if it's not at your farm?"

"Of course!"

Now that I'd found a way to make a difference in Bluefield, I couldn't wait to make an even bigger one.

⁂

The next day, Cat and I went to Helping Hands to drop off another produce donation.

When I hopped out of the truck, I heard a roar and looked up to see a bright red motorcycle pulling in next to us. Marco!

Just then, a blue van rolled up and stopped right next to Marco.

Marco got off his motorcycle. "Right on time!" Marco announced, waving at the van. The door slid open and a little boy scrambled out of it, followed by his sister. I recognized them right away from the *Room Revolutions* videos.

"You're her!" Jack said when he saw me. "The girl who made our attic a playground!"

"The best attic EVER!" the girl added.

A woman climbed out of the van and came over, offering her hand. "I'm Mrs. Mason, and I feel like we're meeting a real celebrity."

144

I felt my face flush. *Me? A CELEBRITY?*

"And what am I?" Marco asked. "The *fake* celebrity?"

"Marco, you're in a class by yourself," her husband said as he unbuckled the twins from their car seats, and we all laughed.

"My kids want to *live* in the attic," Mrs. Mason said. "They don't care if the rest of the house is ever finished." Then she noticed the produce crates in the back of Cat's truck. "Need a hand?"

She and Marco helped us carry the produce into the lobby, where Eileen was waiting. Along with Eli, holding his tablet.

Wait, *what?*

"Okay," I said. "What the heck is going on?"

Marco broke into a huge laugh. He nodded at Eli, who held up his tablet, shooting video.

"Blaire," Mrs. Mason began, putting down the crate of produce. "When Marco showed us the Operation Awesome Sauce video, we were so inspired by how you gathered up your family and classmates to help the food pantry. We're new to Bluefield, but watching everyone work together like that to help their neighbors . . . it made us proud to be part of this town.

"We want to get involved, too. So, we're going to sponsor a kitchen renovation, right here at the Helping Hands Center, so you can have more of these kinds of canning events."

"Oh my goodness," Eileen said, putting her hand to her chest. "Are you serious?"

"Dead serious," Mrs. Mason said. "Marco has generously offered to design it."

"A kitchen right there at the center?" Eileen said breathlessly. "More canning events would be wonderful, and we've talked about offering cooking classes, especially classes where people can train for restaurant jobs. And take-and-bake events for folks to come to assemble large casseroles and bring them home."

"I love it!" Mrs. Mason said.

"I could help you guys make more videos," Eli said. "You know, to spread the word about what you're doing."

Marco turned and smiled. "Of course! *Fantastico* idea."

"What do you think, Blaire?" Marco asked. He must have seen the stunned look on my face.

"I think it's . . . amazing." Then an idea-spark came to me. "Eileen, do you think we could plan a class that's all about cooking with dairy-free ingredients?

And maybe more classes, that deal with other diet restrictions?"

Eileen smiled and said, "Absolutely, Blaire."

"Can you show us your current kitchen space so I can start designing?" Marco asked. Eileen nodded and started leading everyone down the hall. I hung back, still making sense of this amazing news. The center was going to get a kitchen renovation!

Or should I say, *revolution*.

A revolution that was going to change a lot of things, for a lot of people in Bluefield, for the better.

CHAPTER 16

Making the Case

"O kay, kids," the photographer said, "squeeze in a little closer so I get everyone?"

My whole class was seated in front of the COMMUNITY SERVICE ALL-STARS sign in our school lobby. I sat in the first row with Thea and Eli. We were each holding up a jar of Awesome Sauce.

They were from a separate batch I'd made with my mom and Abby.

"Ready to rock?" Ms. Lewis called out from her spot.

"Ready to roll!" we all shouted, and a camera flash went off.

"This looks perfect," said the photographer, checking the display on his camera. "It should run in the paper next week, along with an article about what your students did for Helping Hands."

"Are you guys ready to claim your spot in the case?" Ms. Cheeger asked.

Lots of voices shouted at once. *Oh yeah. So ready! Let's do it!*

Ms. Lewis carried a mason jar over to the case. It was like the ones we'd used, and even had an OPERATION AWESOME SAUCE label and bow on it. But instead of actual sauce, it was filled with red tissue paper and orange, yellow, green, and white paper confetti. Ms. Cheeger had made a sign that said, MS. LEWIS'S FIFTH GRADE 2019–2020, and we'd all signed our names.

Ms. Lewis slid open the case. "Here you go, front and center."

Ms. Cheeger placed the sign in the spot, and Ms. Lewis put the jar of pretend-sauce below it. Then she closed the case and stepped back.

"How's that for our mark on Bluefield Elementary?" I whispered to Thea.

"That jar looks really good next to the picture of George's doghouse," she whispered back.

Hopefully, our display would inspire other students

for their Community Service Challenge projects for years to come.

Just then, a class of younger kids came filing past the lobby. I spotted Abby in the group. She saw me and waved.

"It looks like Abby's forgiven you," Thea said.

I nodded. "We had a great time picking more vegetables and making another batch of sauce."

"Hey, Blaire," Abby called. "Don't forget. My birthday's on Sunday. You owe me lunch!"

I laughed and said, "I remember."

"Abby!" Abby's teacher called from the front of the line. "Stay with the group!"

"Cake, too," Abby called to me before running to catch up with her class.

⁂

Back in our classroom, Ms. Lewis gathered us all on the carpet.

"So, Blaire," Ms. Lewis said. "What will you remember most about this experience?"

Abby's face popped into my head. "The people I've met along the way," I said. Then I thought about Marco. "I'll also remember that helping doesn't have to mean one big, splashy project. Helping means showing up, again and again, until a problem is solved."

"Those are fantastic things for all of us to remember," Ms. Lewis said. "Anyone else want to share?"

Eli raised his hand. He was wearing a T-shirt that just said BLUEFIELD YOUTH SOCCER on it. It looked like he had joined another part of the community.

"I learned that one way you can help others is to just know what they're dealing with," he said. "Whether that's not having enough to eat or feeling sad about something or whatever."

Eli glanced at me.

"That's a great observation, Eli," Ms. Lewis said. "Talking and listening and working together is what people do as a community." Ms. Lewis looked at the clock. "Time to line up for lunch."

I headed to my cubby to get my lunch box. I felt someone tug on my sleeve. It was Eli.

"Hey, what are you doing this weekend?"

"I'm making lunch for someone special," I said.

Then an idea-spark burst in a million colors, and I added:

"But it would be more fun to do it with a friend. Want to come over and cook with me?"

READY TO MAKE SOME OF
BLAIRE'S
FAVORITE RECIPES
YOURSELF?

Keep reading!

A NOTE FROM THE CHEF:

When you see this symbol, ask an adult for help before continuing. Always get a grown-up to help with the stove or burner, sharp objects, and electric appliances, and ask them to check the ingredient lists for allergies before you begin. Don't forget to wash your hands before you start cooking and after handling raw eggs.

Have fun!

—Blaire

AWESOME SAUCE!

Makes 12 servings

INGREDIENTS

¼ cup olive oil

1 cup chopped onion

6 garlic cloves, peeled and minced

1 cup peeled and sliced carrots

1 cup seeded and diced red or green pepper

1 cup diced zucchini

10 cups chopped fresh tomato

Don't forget to wash before chopping!

1 teaspoon salt

1½ teaspoons black pepper

2 teaspoons dried parsley flakes

1 teaspoon dried oregano

1 teaspoon dried basil

Ask an adult to help with the knives, peeler, stove, and boiling sauce.

DIRECTIONS

1. Heat the olive oil in a large saucepan or small stockpot over medium heat. Add the onion, garlic, carrots, pepper, and zucchini. Cook, stirring occasionally, for 6 to 8 minutes, or until vegetables start to soften.

2. Add tomatoes and spices and increase heat to medium-high. Bring mixture to a boil, stirring occasionally. When sauce begins to boil, reduce heat to low and simmer for 2 hours, stirring occasionally. For a smoother sauce, simmer for 2½ hours.

3. Remove from heat. Sauce may be used right away or stored in the refrigerator for up to 2 weeks. To freeze, let sauce cool completely before transferring to freezer-safe containers.

4. Serve sauce over your favorite pasta.

Make sure you store the sauce
in the fridge or freezer.

aka Crispy Green Bean Fries!

FOREST GIANT FINGERS

Serves 4

INGREDIENTS

Olive oil spray

¾ cup breadcrumbs

1½ tablespoons seasoning blend (such as Italian seasoning)

¼ teaspoon salt

¼ teaspoon pepper

2 eggs

1 pound fresh green beans

Or you can use zucchini cut into sticks!

✋ **Ask an adult to help with the oven and kitchen tongs.**

DIRECTIONS

1. Preheat oven to 425 degrees. Lightly spray a baking sheet with olive oil spray.

2. Combine breadcrumbs, seasoning blend, salt, and pepper in a medium bowl.

3. Use a kitchen shears to trim off the ends of the green beans. Rinse beans and shake off excess water.

4. Break the eggs into a shallow bowl and beat with a fork.

5. Dip the green beans, one at a time, into the egg, then transfer to the bowl of breadcrumbs. Use a spoon to sprinkle the beans with the breadcrumb mixture. Place the beans on the baking sheet, leaving space between them.

6. Spray the beans lightly with olive oil spray. Have an adult put the baking sheet in the oven.

7. Bake for 10 minutes. Have an adult remove the sheet from the oven. Use kitchen tongs to turn the green beans over. Have an adult put the sheet back into the oven.

8. Bake another 3 to 5 minutes or until the beans are crisp.

9. Try the beans with a dipping sauce, such as ranch dressing or marinara.

(Pssst! Awesome Sauce makes a great dip!)

My new favorite dessert!

ELI'S DAIRY-FREE CHOCOLATE CHIP BROWNIES

Makes 24 brownies

INGREDIENTS

Cooking spray

1 cup vegetable oil

1 cup maple syrup

½ cup soy milk

1 tablespoon vanilla

2 cups flour

1 cup cocoa

1½ cups sugar

2 tablespoons baking powder

½ teaspoon salt

1 cup dairy-free chocolate chips*

✋ **Ask an adult to help with the oven.**

DIRECTIONS

1. Preheat oven to 350 degrees. Spray a 9x13 baking pan with cooking spray.

2. Combine the oil, maple syrup, soy milk, and vanilla in a large bowl. Mix with a whisk.

3. In a separate bowl, combine the flour, cocoa, sugar, baking powder, and salt.

4. Add the dry ingredients to the wet ingredients and mix just until combined. Gently fold in the chocolate chips. Pour the batter into the baking pan.

5. Bake for 30 to 35 minutes or until a toothpick inserted in the center comes out clean.

6. Have an adult remove the pan from the oven. Let the brownies cool completely before cutting into squares.

*Enjoy Life is one brand of allergy-friendly chocolate chips.

ABOUT THE AUTHOR

Jennifer Castle grew up writing stories in her head on long school bus rides and was constantly looking for ways to turn her idea-sparks into reality. These included dozens of poems, a homemade magazine that lasted three issues, a barrette-making business, and a cruise boat made of branches and cardboard for the creek behind her house. Eventually, one of her "big ideas" became a published novel, and since then she has written more than ten books for kids and teens, including the Butterfly Wishes series, *Together at Midnight*, and *Famous Friends*. Jennifer lives among the mountains, woods, and bountiful farms of New York's Hudson Valley with her husband, two daughters, and two striped cats, who also work part-time as her writing assistants.

SPECIAL THANKS

With gratitude to Lindsey Lusher Shute, Executive Director and Co-founder of the National Young Farmers Coalition and co-owner of Hearty Roots Community Farm in New York's Hudson Valley; Dr. Amanda Cox, Assistant Professor of Pediatrics in the Division of Pediatric Allergy and Immunology and fellow of the American Academy of Allergy, Asthma, and Immunology; Dr. Megan Moreno, Academic Division Chief: General Pediatrics and Adolescent Medicine, Vice Chair of Digital Health, and Principal Investigator of the Social Media and Adolescent Health Research Team (SMAHRT); and Kamille Adamany, Director of Restaurants at American Girl, for their insights and knowledge.

Ready to
COOK UP more
FUN with
Blaire?

VISIT
*americangirl.com to learn more
about Blaire's world!*

Parents, request a FREE catalogue at
americangirl.com/catalogue

Sign up at **americangirl.com/email**
to receive the latest news and exclusive offers

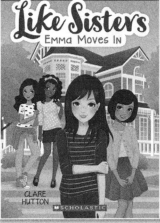

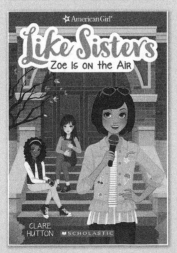
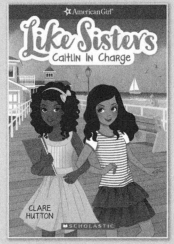